Things are getting "out of hand" . . .

The package was small and roughly cylindrical, and had been wrapped in heavy brown paper and tied with string.

"What's that?" Carson asked, pausing briefly in extolling the virtues of his plan.

"I don't know," Pickett said, pulling one end of the string until the knot came free. "Our hostess said it had been left for me. At least, I *think* that's what she said."

"Who would even know we were going to be here?" Thomas wondered aloud. "We sure didn't, until two days ago."

Pickett offered no opinion on the subject. He unrolled the tube of brown paper until it disgorged its contents— whereupon his expressive countenance changed color. He uttered a strangled sound, dropping the item and its wrappings to the floor as he ran from the inn.

"What—gorblimey!" Thomas exclaimed, his face assuming a greenish cast as Carson bent to retrieve the object and hold it up for their inspection.

It was just over two inches in length and, like its wrappings, roughly cylindrical in shape. Its color was a mottled gray, although at one time it had very likely been nearer to pink.

It was, in fact, a human finger.

THE JOHN PICKETT MYSTERIES:

PICKPOCKET'S APPRENTICE
(prequel novella)

IN MILADY'S CHAMBER

A DEAD BORE

FAMILY PLOT

DINNER MOST DEADLY

WAITING GAME
(Christmas novella)

TOO HOT TO HANDEL

FOR DEADER OR WORSE

MYSTERY LOVES COMPANY

PERIL BY POST

INTO THIN EIRE

Into Thin Eire

Another John Pickett Mystery

Sheri Cobb South

1

*In Which John Pickett
Receives an Offer He Can't Refuse*

M agistrate wants you."

To John Pickett, met with this greeting as he entered the Bow Street Public Office one Monday morning in July, it was amazing that those three simple words still had the power to send a swarm of butterflies cavorting about in his stomach, even after almost six years of service with the Bow Street force.

"Told me to send you in as soon as you arrived," continued Dixon, the senior principal officer at more than twice Pickett's age of five-and-twenty. He jerked a callused thumb in the direction of Patrick Colquhoun's office.

"Yes—thank you—I'll go to him at once," Pickett stammered, uncomfortably aware of half a dozen stares aimed in his direction, from Mr. Dixon's mild blue gaze to the unconcealed curiosity of two members of the Foot Patrol, looking up from their perusal of the latest issue of the *Hue and*

Cry. Even the knowing smirk of Harry Carson, Horse Patrol man and the bane of Pickett's existence, was absent on this occasion.

It wasn't that Pickett was afraid of Mr. Colquhoun—at least, not any longer, although the scrawny fourteen-year-old who had once been hauled before the bench for pinching an apple from a costermonger in Covent Garden certainly had been. No, his only fear these days (at least, his only fear where the magistrate was concerned) was that of being a disappointment, of proving himself to be unworthy of the interest Mr. Colquhoun had taken in him. To his knowledge, he hadn't done anything deserving of censure since the botched business in the Lake District a month earlier—and Mr. Colquhoun had been adamant in absolving him of any blame in that. A furtive glance at the large clock mounted on the wall behind the bench assured him that he wasn't late. What, then—?

No answer came to him in the short time it took him to reach the door of the magistrate's office. Pickett took a deep breath, set his shoulders, and rapped on the doorframe, then, upon being instructed by a voice from inside to come in, pushed the door open.

Mr. Colquhoun stood there, an energetic Scotsman some sixty-four years of age, with thick white hair and brilliant blue eyes. But he was not alone. A man was with him, a middle-aged man whose receding hair was nevertheless fashionably cropped and curled, and who wore the blue and buff colors favored by the Whig party in general and the Prince of Wales in particular. And gold braid. So *much* gold braid. Whoever this man was, he was someone very important. *Which means that whatever it is I've done,* Pickett thought miserably, *it must have been something* very *bad.*

He turned to address the magistrate with a silent question in his eyes. Mr. Colquhoun, usually not shy about letting his feelings be known, was singularly uncommunicative on this occasion. In fact, if Pickett had not known better, he would have sworn the magistrate was as dazed as he was himself.

"I—er—Mr. Dixon said you wanted me, sir."

"Aye, come in and shut the door."

Pickett obeyed, and Mr. Colquhoun gestured toward his visitor. "This is Lord Fortescue, Gentleman of the Bedchamber to the Prince of Wales."

Pickett never would have presumed to offer his hand to such a personage, but upon seeing the personage extend a hand in his direction, he took it.

"It's a pleasure to meet you, Mr. Pickett. I confess, I had expected to see someone rather older."

"Oh?" was all Pickett could manage. The inevitable reference to his age paled beside the implication that anyone so highly placed in the prince's household might have any expectations regarding him at all.

"Word of your recent heroics has reached the ears of His Royal Highness," continued the prince's emissary.

"My—my recent—"

"In the Lake District," the man explained. "And although His Royal Highness recognizes that much of what happened there will never be made known to the public, he wishes me to express his gratitude for your actions on behalf of king and country."

"As to that, your lordship, it wasn't exactly—" Upon seeing the magistrate fix a warning look upon him, Pickett faltered into silence.

"Yes, yes, I'm sure your humility does you credit," the prince's man said, dismissing Pickett's objections with an impatient wave of his hand. "But now to the purpose of my visit. As you may be aware, the king's health in recent years has not been good."

And that, Pickett thought, was an understatement if ever he'd heard one. George III's periodic bouts of madness were surely the worst-kept secret in the kingdom, and had been since before Pickett was born. Among the more lurid tales were accounts of the king's chasing the novelist Fanny Burney about Kew Gardens in an attempt to kiss her, or trying to shake hands with a tree in the firm belief that it was the King of Prussia.

"The question of a Regency is, I fear, no longer a matter of 'if,' but of 'when'," Lord Fortescue continued.

"Oh?" Pickett asked, not sure what any of this had to do with his "heroics"—he could think of a better word for them—in the Lake District.

"But the political views of His Royal Highness are poles apart from his father's. There are those who do not want to see the prince take the reins of government a day sooner than he must."

"Er, no, I suppose not," Pickett said, seeing some response was called for.

"Just so, Mr. Pickett. It is even possible that some radical might be tempted to, let us say, remove the threat, thinking His Majesty's second son, the Duke of York, might be easier to manage."

"Oh?" Pickett asked again.

"That being the case, His Royal Highness believes it might be wise to retain the services of a personal bodyguard. Not merely an escort when he goes out, as Bow Street's own Mr. Townsend used to do, but a man on the premises around the clock. That, Mr. Pickett, is where you come in."

"Me?" Pickett echoed intelligently.

"I am authorized to offer you a position as personal bodyguard to His Royal Highness the Prince of Wales, at a salary of five hundred pounds per annum."

His jaw dropped, and Pickett, suddenly aware of his gaping mouth, shut it with an effort, cleared his throat, and opened it again. "You—you want *me* to—to—" The very idea was so absurd that he could hardly find words with which to express it.

"Perhaps I was not clear," his lordship demurred hastily. "The offer does not come from me, but from His Royal Highness. In addition to the salary I have named, you will also have rooms at Carlton House for yourself and your wife—Mr. Colquhoun told me before you arrived that you were recently married, is that correct?—and I believe a knighthood at some future date is not beyond the realm of possibility, although I can of course make no promises; such things are not in His Royal Highness's purview, unless and until he becomes Regent."

Pickett could only stare at him. "I—I—I—"

The prince's emissary, eyeing Pickett's brown serge coat with disfavor, bethought himself of one caveat. "Mind you, His Royal Highness is not called the First Gentleman of Europe for nothing. He holds himself, and all those around him, to a certain standard of appearance, and you would be no exception. He has taken it upon himself to design new uniforms for the 10th Hussar regiment, and already has plans in mind for the costume of his personal bodyguard as well."

"As it happens," put in Mr. Colquhoun, seeing his most junior Runner at a loss, "Mr. Pickett will be leaving London early tomorrow morning. Perhaps you might discuss the matter with him in more detail after he returns, by which time he may have thought of questions he wishes to put to you."

"Of course," agreed the visitor, who in truth was having some difficulty reconciling the accounts of bravery and heroism which had reached the prince's ears with the rather gauche and inarticulate young man who stood before him.

"Well, John," Mr. Colquhoun said, after seeing his exalted visitor off the premises and returning to his office, where Pickett still stood as if turned to stone, "it appears you'll soon be leaving us."

"You—you knew about this, sir?" Pickett turned to regard the magistrate much as a drowning man might regard a lifeline thrown from a passing ship.

Mr. Colquhoun shook his head. "Not until just before you did."

"He said it was because of that business in the Lake District, but it wasn't at all like he seems to think! I can't take such a position under false pretenses."

"I'm sure your scruples do you credit, John, but it seems to me that the Crown—or, in this case, the man who may very soon be its representative—is unlikely to be particular about *how* a treasonous plot is stopped, just so long as it *is* stopped."

"Then—then you think I should accept."

The magistrate's bushy white eyebrows drew together across the bridge of his nose. "Some might say you'd be a fool to refuse! You're unlikely to get another such opportunity."

"I—I had no thought of leaving Bow Street, sir. I owe you a debt of gratitude—"

"Which was paid in full long ago." Seeing his young protégé was not convinced, he added, "Make no mistake, John. You have a position here for as long as you want it. I should be genuinely sorry to see you go, but I'm not so selfish that I could keep you here against your own best interests."

"Did you hear what he said? About a knighthood, I mean. That would make Julia—"

"Lady Pickett," concluded the magistrate, nodding. "But let me point out that she would not be the one charged with the task of protecting the prince's royal person. Nor, for that matter, does she seem to have any objections to being plain 'Mrs. John Pickett.' I don't say her wishes shouldn't be considered, for her life would change as much as yours as a result of your joining the prince's household. But if you're thinking to accept the offer for such a reason as that, I should caution you against it. After all, the man said himself that he can make no promises."

Pickett sighed. "No, sir. Thank you for buying me a little time, anyway." A hint of a smile went some way toward dispelling his dazed expression. "Should I go into hiding for the next fortnight, while I'm supposedly out of London?"

"There'll be no need for that," the magistrate assured him, picking up a creased sheet of paper that lay on his desk and handing it to Pickett. "I spoke no less than the truth when I said you'd be leaving London in the morning. This came in the morning post, requesting two Runners—yourself and one other, the second man left to my own choosing—to be sent to Dunbury on a matter of some delicacy."

" 'A matter of some delicacy,' " Pickett echoed bitterly. "Just once, I'd like someone to say what he wants."

"At least he signed his name." Clearly, the magistrate, too, was thinking of the anonymous summons that had brought Pickett to the Lake District, also for an unspecified purpose. Sure enough, the letter was signed by one Edward Gaines Brockton, giving as his address the Cock and Boar in Dunbury.

"Where is Dunbury?" Pickett asked, looking up from the letter. "And who do you intend to send with me?"

"Dunbury is in the West Country. Somersetshire, to be exact—not far from your in-laws, in fact. As for your traveling companion, I was thinking of sending Mr. Carson."

"*Harry?*" The thought of Harry Carson as a traveling companion was enough to drive all thoughts of the Prince of Wales from Pickett's brain, at least temporarily.

The bushy eyebrows rose. "You have some objection?"

"You must do as you think best, sir, but—but Harry's in the Horse Patrol!"

"Think, John," chided his mentor. "If I do as this man

asks and send another Runner with you, that's two of the six—fully one-third of Bow Street's principal officers at any given time, and forty percent at present, since I haven't yet named a replacement for Mr. Foote. We're already one man short, and may soon be two, if you decide to accept His Royal Highness's offer."

By which observation Pickett could only assume that his mentor was considering Harry Carson as a candidate for principal officer. Still, he knew better than to ask; the promotion of men from the patrols to principal officer was left solely to the magistrate's discretion, and Mr. Colquhoun would take issue—and rightfully so—with any suggestion that he should be accountable to any of the existing Runners, least of all the youngest of the lot, for the naming of their fellows.

"Do you know anything against Mr. Carson that would disqualify him for the position?" asked Mr. Colquhoun, reading Pickett's thoughts with reasonable accuracy as they flitted across his expressive countenance.

"N-no," Pickett conceded. He knew of nothing against Harry, except for the fact that he himself was all too often the butt of the fellow's jokes.

"Who would you suggest I send instead?" Mr. Colquhoun persisted.

Since he had been invited, more or less, to voice an opinion, Pickett considered the matter. Mr. Dixon was fifty years old, and had been with Bow Street longer than Pickett had been alive, having joined the Foot Patrol in the days of no less a personage than Sir John Fielding. No one could doubt

Dixon's competence, and yet Pickett could not help feeling that, if Mr. Colquhoun were to send Dixon with him, it would be John Pickett who would end up assisting Mr. Dixon, rather than the other way 'round. Maxwell seemed like a good man, but Pickett didn't know him well, as he had come to Bow Street only recently after being invalided out of the army. Griffin was currently working a case of his own, and Marshall was in Yorkshire on assignment.

"I didn't mean to suggest that I couldn't work with Carson," Pickett said at last, having failed to come up with a more acceptable alternative. He was forced to admit that it might have been a great deal worse: after all, he'd even managed to work with Mr. Foote, and he did Harry Carson the justice to own that Carson, at least, had no desire to see him hang for stealing an apple (among other things) in his misspent youth. Then again, perhaps Harry Carson was unaware of his inglorious past. Or maybe he simply hadn't thought of it yet. Either way, there was only one response Pickett could make. "Whoever you may choose to send with me, sir, he will have my best efforts. So will you, come to that."

Mr. Colquhoun nodded in approval. "Somehow I expected no less from you."

"Er, I do have one question, though," Pickett added hesitantly.

"Do you, now? And what is that, Mr. Pickett?"

"Well, sir, given that Carson is a member of the Horse Patrol, I don't suppose—that is, you won't expect me to—what I mean to say, sir—"

Mr. Colquhoun listened to this disjointed speech with unholy glee for some minutes before putting Pickett out of his misery. "Never fear, Mr. Pickett, the two of you will be traveling by stage. I don't expect you to make a two-day journey on horseback."

Pickett breathed a sigh of relief. "No, sir. Thank you, sir."

"I never did hold with cruelty to dumb animals—and the horse probably wouldn't like it, either," continued the magistrate, drawing a sheepish grin from Pickett. "Now, if you'll fetch Mr. Carson, we'll inform him of his new assignment before I send you home to pack your bags and inform your wife of your sudden rise in the world. I refer, of course, to His Royal Highness, not to a protracted visit to Dunbury in Mr. Carson's company."

Pickett did as he was bidden, and a moment later Harry Carson burst upon the magistrate's office, a handsome fellow a couple of years older than Pickett himself, clad in the blue coat and red waistcoat of the Bow Street Horse Patrol. "Yes, sir?" he asked Mr. Colquhoun. "Lord John said you wanted to see me?"

Pickett refused to take the bait, but gave the magistrate a speaking look nevertheless. Mr. Colquhoun did not acknowledge this by so much as the flicker of an eyelid, but addressed himself instead to Carson. "A letter arrived in this morning's post, requesting that I send Mr. Pickett along with another principal officer. As we are shorthanded at the moment, I had thought to send you instead. Tell me, what do you make of this?"

He handed the letter to the man who was Pickett's junior

in everything but years. Carson studied it for a long moment before giving it back to the magistrate with a shrug. "I should say someone named Edward Gaines Brockton needs a couple of Runners in Dunbury, although I can't imagine why one wouldn't suffice. Besides that, there's really not much to go on, is there?"

"Mr. Pickett?"

As he took the letter from his magistrate's hand, Pickett realized he was being given the opportunity to put his tormentor in his place, and resolved not to let it go to waste. He took a deep breath. "Before Mr. Carson joined us, sir, I asked you where Dunbury was, and you told me it was in the West Country." Pickett would not pretend to prior knowledge he had not possessed, but that didn't mean he couldn't point out, however indirectly, Harry Carson's failure to ask. "Given the distance involved, the fact that it was delivered this morning would seem to indicate that it was mailed the day before yesterday—assuming, of course, that it was sent from Dunbury, and not from some other location."

"A valid point, Mr. Pickett, but probably a safe assumption," Mr. Colquhoun said, acknowledging it with a nod. "Have you any other observations?"

"The quality of the paper suggests that this Mr. Brockton is a man of means," Pickett continued, "but one without connections amongst the aristocracy, given the lack of a frank. A member of the gentry, perhaps, or a well-to-do merchant. As for the contents, there's no way of knowing until we meet with the fellow. 'A matter of some delicacy' might mean anything from a death under suspicious circumstances to a daughter who has eloped with a fortune-hunter."

"Not bad," remarked Carson, cocking one eyebrow at the younger man who was his superior at Bow Street. "Keep it up, and you might amount to something by the time you grow up, Mr. Pickett."

Pickett thought of the position awaiting him, with living quarters in Carlton House and the possibility of a knighthood at some future date, and gave Carson a rather smug smile. "That's 'Lord John' to you."

* * *

Pickett's thoughts took a very different turn, however, after he left the Bow Street Public Office and set out for the Bolt in Tun in Fleet Street, where he paid fares for two passengers to Wells, the stagecoach stop nearest the village of Dunbury, before heading home to Curzon Street. In spite of the good news he had to impart, his steps began to flag as he approached the modest but elegant Mayfair residence. Granted, he liked the *idea* of the position he was being offered—to rise, in less than a dozen years, from picking pockets in Covent Garden to having rooms in the royal residence of the Prince of Wales was heady stuff, and Pickett would be lying if he said the prospect held no appeal. Then, too, it would be highly gratifying to be able to offer his wife a title—not so high a title as the one she had held before marrying him, it was true, but a title nonetheless.

The reality of such a change, however, was a very different matter. For one thing, he was not at all sure he deserved to be rewarded for his actions in the Lake District. Indeed, he could not think of those events for very long without feeling sick to his stomach. There was also the matter of the work he would be called upon to do. Every day at Bow Street brought something new and unexpected—and, occasionally, dangerous. Not that he enjoyed putting his life in jeopardy, precisely, especially now that he had a wife and a child on the way. Still, it kept him on his toes—not unlike the criminal days of his youth, in fact, but with the satisfaction of knowing that he now worked on the right side of the law.

But this new position, if he chose to accept it, entailed one task, and one task alone: protecting the portly person of His Royal Highness, the Prince of Wales. He had never met the prince, of course—even Mr. Colquhoun, wealthy as he was, didn't move in such rarified circles as that. And although Pickett had seen His Royal Highness on one occasion, across Drury Lane Theatre on the night it had burned, his attention on that occasion had all been for Julia, Lady Fieldhurst, and the marriage which they had both fully expected to be annulled.

Still, one did not have to be acquainted with the prince, or even to move in the highest circles, to have heard the rumors that swirled about him: his profligate spending habits and the largely unsuccessful attempts of Parliament to rein him in by controlling his purse-strings; his youthful (and quite unlawful) marriage to the twice-widowed Roman Catholic Maria Fitzherbert, and his legal but disastrous marriage to Princess Caroline of Brunswick, from whom he had been estranged for more than a decade; his susceptibility to flattery from those who hoped to sway his opinions; and, finally, his string of aristocratic mistresses, whose husbands were apparently fully cognizant of their wives' illicit connections with the prince. In fact, it would be difficult to summon any degree of respect, still less admiration, for his prospective employer.

On the other hand, Pickett reasoned, his present position often required him to seek justice for murdered men who had been less than admirable while they were alive—his wife's first husband and her former brother-in-law among them. If a dead man, whatever his defects of character, was deserving of Pickett's best efforts, then surely a living one was no less worthy. Granted, Pickett had never been obliged to live beneath the roof of any of those dead men, to say nothing of being wholly at their beck and call—or being obliged to wear a uniform of their design, he reflected, remembering with distaste the yellow boots of the 10th Hussars, and the contempt with which these were regarded by the other regiments. Still, he would be well paid—*lavishly* paid, in fact—for the loss of personal autonomy, and the possibility of laying a more exalted title at Mrs. John Pickett's feet, especially in the light of all she had given up in order to be with him, was a powerful motivator.

And so it was that, upon arriving at Curzon Street, he waited only long enough to greet his wife of four months with a lingering kiss before asking, "You'd like being married to Sir John Pickett, wouldn't you?"

2

In Which John Pickett Prepares for a Journey

J ulia had discovered early in their acquaintance that her young Bow Street Runner possessed an appealingly self-deprecating sense of humor, and four months of marriage had only reinforced this conviction. That being the case, it seemed oddly out of character, his apparently laying claim to a knighthood. Or was he referring to an imaginary baronetcy? She regarded him for a long moment, studying his face for some clue as to the nature of the jest (for jest it surely must be) before saying, "I like being married to *you*, no matter what you may choose to call yourself."

"But you'd like to be Lady Pickett, wouldn't you?" he persisted. "Granted, it wouldn't be so exalted a title as Lady Fieldhurst, but it beats plain 'Mrs. Pickett' all hollow, doesn't it?"

"I will not allow you to denigrate 'Mrs. Pickett,' " she protested, giving the lapels of his coat a possessive little tug. "I've become rather fond of her. But John, darling, pray cease funning and tell me what you are talking about!"

"I'm not funning," he insisted. He told her, then, all about the unexpected visitor to Bow Street and his incredible errand, concluding with, "It sounds like someone's idea of a joke, doesn't it?"

The news had been enough to make her extricate herself from his embrace so that she might sit down somewhat unsteadily on the nearby sofa, but at this question, she came fiercely to his defense. "Not at all! Why should you *not* be given such an opportunity? Who would be better qualified, pray?"

Someone who hasn't been responsible, however unintentionally, for a woman's death, Pickett might have told her. Aloud, however, he merely cautioned, "He never made any promises about the knighthood, mind you. Still, even if it never comes to pass, the rest of it—the five hundred quid a year and rooms in the royal residence—well, that's nothing to sneeze at, is it?"

"Not at all," she assured him warmly. "Although I feel I must warn you that, if you found this house overwhelming, only wait until you see the grand staircase at Carlton House."

He winced. "That's what I'm afraid of."

"In all seriousness, John"—she rose from the sofa and laid an imploring hand on his arm—"if you don't want to take the position, don't feel you must do so on my account. I haven't the slightest objection to remaining 'Mrs. John Pickett' for the rest of my life. Indeed, I expected nothing less when we married."

" 'Nothing less'?" he echoed, seizing upon the

expression as he took her into his arms. "I didn't think there *was* anything less."

"That is a matter of opinion," she informed him, lifting her face to be kissed.

He was happy to oblige, but felt compelled to ask, upon completion of this pleasant exercise, "My lady, have I ever told you that you have very poor judgment?"

"Many times. Still, I have no regrets. Well," she amended, "only one regret, in any case."

This criticism, mild though it was, was sufficient to wipe the smile from his face. "Oh? What—?"

"I shall always regret that I never had a proper proposal of marriage from you."

"Did you not?" he asked in some consternation. "Surely I must have—"

"As I recall, you were too busy enumerating for me all the reasons why I could not possibly wish to marry you."

This claim held an undeniable ring of truth. Aside from the fact that his memories of the event were vague, given that he had been recovering from a head injury at the time, it still seemed strange, even after four months of marriage to think that she, a viscountess, could fall in love with a Bow Street Runner, let alone want to marry him. "I'm glad you didn't listen, anyway," he said, seeing some response was called for.

"Of course, it's never too late," she observed.

"What do you mean?"

She regarded him expectantly. "You could make me an offer of marriage now."

He gave a little laugh, hoping she was funning, but very

much afraid she was not. He could think of few things that would make him feel more foolish than the idea of going down on one knee to offer marriage to a woman who was already his wife—a woman, moreover, who was four months gone with child. "It's a little late for that, don't you think?"

Her thoughts must have been running along very similar lines, for she pressed one hand to her abdomen. The gentle swell was still concealed by her skirts, at least for now, but that state of affairs was growing more precarious by the day. "It isn't as if I can turn you down, you know."

"In all seriousness, Julia, I didn't come home just to tell you about the prince's offer," Pickett said, changing the subject with some relief. "I have to pack my bags. I'll be leaving London first thing in the morning."

"Oh," she said, somewhat daunted by this revelation. In an effort to lessen the bleakness that threatened to descend upon her at the prospect of his absence, she added in a lighter tone, "Surely it isn't necessary to go to such lengths as all that, merely to avoid making me a proposal of marriage."

His smile flickered briefly, but he said only, "I wish I could take you with me, but I'm afraid I can't. The letter requested two men, so instead of my beautiful and clever wife, I'm stuck with Harry Carson of the Horse Patrol."

"What's wrong with Harry Carson?"

"Other than the fact that he's not you? I don't suppose there's anything 'wrong with' him, exactly. It's just that he seems to consider everything a joke—and few jokes are funnier than the idea of me, married to a lady."

"Is he the one who dubbed you 'Lord John' then?" Upon

receiving an answer in the affirmative, she urged, "Pay him no heed! It is obvious to the meanest intelligence that he is jealous."

"It's certainly obvious that he has reason to be." He drew her into his arms and propped his chin on the top of her head, resting it in a nest of golden curls. "But there's no reason why you should stay here alone, you know. I'll be in Dunbury, not so very far from your parents. If you'd like to go to them, I might be able to ride over to see you from time to time."

She could not read the expression on his face, as her own face was buried in his chest, but a slight stiffening of the figure in her arms, as well as something in the offhand manner in which he had spoken, suggested there was more to this offer than might at first appear. Still, she spoke in a jesting tone that matched his, trusting that he would confide in her when he was ready to do so—and not one minute before. "Ride? My dear John! Are you truly offering to come to me on horseback? I am quite overcome! But I seem to recall your telling me once that you could be back in London before all the plans for my own travel were in place."

"Yes, but then I knew what I was looking for—or at least, I was reasonably sure that I would know it if I saw it," he amended. "But I don't know how long I may be gone this time. It might be a fortnight or more."

"Two days will be too long, let alone two weeks," she said, releasing him with some reluctance. "Still, I daresay it won't be the last time you will be obliged to travel, so I might as well accustom myself to being on my own. Besides, I had thought to entertain a few ladies to tea. Not a large party, you understand, only a few acquaintances from before my marriage—before *our* marriage, I should say."

Her own studied nonchalance would have instantly aroused Pickett's suspicions, had his mind been less troubled. "I don't like leaving you alone," he confessed.

"I shall hardly be alone in a house full of servants," she pointed out.

"Not quite full, I'm afraid. I'm going to have to take Thomas with me. I've put the fellow off too many times already."

"He'll be over the moon," she predicted.

She was quite right.

"I—I'm to come with you, sir?" Thomas stammered, upon being informed that he was not only to pack his master's bag for the journey, but to accompany him on his travels.

"Yes. Mind you, it's only to Dunbury," Pickett added, seeing that his valet, recently promoted from footman, appeared to be laboring under the delusion that he was about to embark upon the Grand Tour. "It's not as if we're going to Paris or Rome."

"It might as well be to me, for I've never gone beyond Hampstead. Not that I've any particular wish to visit a place full of frogs or dagos in any case," he added hastily, apparently fearful that his loyalty to his homeland might be called into question by his apparent eagerness to leave it.

"There is one other thing," Pickett cautioned. "I won't be traveling alone."

"Will Mrs. Pickett be coming with us, then?"

Pickett sighed. "No, not Mrs. Pickett, but another man

from Bow Street. His name is Harry Carson. Most Bow Street Runners don't travel with servants"—*Most Bow Street Runners can't afford them*, he might have added—"so I'm afraid you may be obliged to do for him as well as for me."

"I'll do my best not to disappoint, sir," Thomas declared stoutly, then moved to the clothespress and began extracting the garments Pickett might require for an extended sojourn. He hesitated over a dark blue tailcoat and a waistcoat of white brocade. "Will you require anything for evening wear, sir?"

Pickett hesitated. It was true that he'd attended evening entertainments while investigating previous cases, but he'd been accompanied by his wife on those occasions. In fact, it had been Julia who had given him the *entrée*; Harry Carson's presence was unlikely to produce the same effect. Moreover, Carson's response were he to discover such garments in Pickett's bag (much less upon his person) Pickett could only too easily imagine. On the other hand, he would—as he'd pointed out to Julia—be within reasonable riding distance of her parents. If Julia should happen to write to them, mentioning his presence in the vicinity, would they feel it incumbent upon them to invite him to dinner? If so, he would be obligated to accept, and he refused to give Lady Runyon further reason to despise him by appearing at her dinner table in his boots.

"Best pack it, just in case," he told Thomas, who was clearly awaiting an answer. "I may not need it, but I suppose it's better to be prepared."

"Yes, sir," Thomas said, although whether this was in obedience or agreement, Pickett could not be sure.

Once his valet was embarked upon the task of packing his things, Pickett turned his attention to one additional arrangement necessary to his comfort, and to this end, sought out Rogers, the butler.

"Rogers, I shall be obliged to leave London first thing in the morning," he began.

"Yes, sir. So I had heard," the butler said, leaving Pickett to wonder (not for the first time) how servants managed to know everything that went on in the house almost as soon as it occurred.

He had not long to consider the matter, however, for he had more important things on his mind. He glanced around the hall to make sure Julia was not within earshot. He saw no sign of her, but lowered his voice nevertheless. "Tell me, Rogers, do you know how to use a firearm?"

If Rogers found this question at all surprising, he did not betray it by so much as the flicker of an eyelash. "I do, sir."

"There is a pistol in the bottom drawer of the bureau," Pickett told him. "Don't hesitate to make use of it, if you should need it."

"No, sir, but—begging your pardon, but is there any reason why you should think some form of defense might be necessary?"

"I—I don't like leaving Julia alone," Pickett confessed.

Manfully overlooking his master's *faux pas* in referring to the mistress of the house by her Christian name in front of the staff, Rogers permitted himself an avuncular smile. "I'm sure your sentiments do you credit, sir, but I can assure you that Mrs. Pickett will not be entirely alone."

"No, of course not," Pickett agreed, dismissing his qualms with a shake of his head. After all, the man he feared was in prison, awaiting execution. For all he knew, the fellow might already have kept his appointment with the hangman, and word had not yet reached Mr. Colquhoun, who had requested to be informed of the event. Or perhaps it had, and Mr. Colquhoun—a busy man with many interests in addition to his duties as a magistrate—had merely forgotten to pass the information along to him. He wished he had made inquiries before leaving Bow Street, but it was too late now. "Pay me no heed, Rogers. I suppose I'm being foolish."

"If I may say so, sir, it is a foolishness that has done Mrs. Pickett a great deal of good, and one that has considerably endeared you to the staff."

"Thank you, Rogers." Pickett gave the butler a grateful, if self-conscious, little smile, and returned to the bedchamber to finish his packing.

But much later that night, upon completion of a very protracted and private farewell, he felt compelled to say, "Julia, you will be careful, won't you? Take care of yourself, I mean. Don't go out alone. If you must go anywhere, take Betsy with you, or the new footman—the fellow who replaced Thomas—what was his name again?"

"Andrew. And if it will make you feel any better, I promise not to leave the house without one or the other," she added, laying a protective hand on the gentle swell of her abdomen in the mistaken assumption that this sudden concern on his part was due to her delicate condition. He might have informed her of her error, but the bedroom was dark and so he could not see the gesture. "Better still, I shall take both. Then, too, I can invite Rogers to come along, and I shall parade through London like Good Queen Bess going on progress."

"Julia—" he protested feebly.

"Never mind, darling, I was only funning." In a more serious vein, she added, "I know you must go, and I promise not to beg you to stay, or tease you to take me with you, or plague you with a show of tears, but am I allowed to say that I shall miss you?"

"I hope so," he said, reaching for her again, "because I'll miss you. Very, very much."

3

Which Introduces Mr. Harry Carson
of the Bow Street Horse Patrol

P ickett arose before dawn and reached for the clothes which he'd allowed Thomas to lay out for him the night before. The fact that he had to grope in the darkness before locating them was, in his estimation, further proof of the advantages of performing such tasks for oneself rather than leaving them to a manservant, but he had long since yielded to Julia in the matter, and had been rewarded so sweetly for his capitulation that the inconvenience of fumbling for his clothes had seemed a very small price to pay. He wondered if she now felt the game had not been worth the candle; a rustling of the sheets beside him gave him to understand that his search had not been conducted as quietly as he might have wished.

"I didn't mean to awaken you," he said in an apologetic whisper. "Go back to sleep, and I'll see you when I return."

"And when will that be?" she retorted a bit sleepily. "I

intend to spend every moment I can with you until you are obliged to leave, so you might as well save your breath."

It was exactly the response he had expected—and, in truth, he would have been disappointed in anything less—so he made no attempt to persuade her. Having dressed, shaved, and packed the last of his things in a battered valise, he ushered Julia out of the room. Together they descended the stairs to the breakfast room, where Julia had instructed the cook the night before to set out a selection of pastries. Conversation was desultory; Julia was not a creature of matutinal habits even at the best of times, but quite aside from the early hour, both were too conscious of the approaching separation to incline either toward loquaciousness.

"What time will you reach Dunbury?" Julia asked at last, feeling some attempt at normality was in order.

"Tomorrow afternoon, barring any accident on the road. Tonight we'll be stopping in Reading." He gave her a reminiscent little smile. "I don't expect to enjoy it as much as I did my last stay there."

"Oh?" she challenged him. "And just how much to you remember about your last stay there? As I recall, I was obliged to dose you with laudanum as soon as we reached our room, and you fell asleep almost as soon as your head hit the pillow—hardly the wedding night every woman dreams of."

"Let me point out that an extended visit to his new in-laws is hardly the honeymoon every man dreams of, either," he responded in kind.

In fact, neither of their recollections told the whole tale, for the wedding Julia spoke of was essentially a legal protection, necessary only insofar as it prevented her first husband's influential family from nullifying the marriage by declaration they had unintentionally formed in Scotland some three months earlier. As for the honeymoon, they had enjoyed a week of wedded bliss in Pickett's Drury Lane flat before the legal ceremony and the trip to her parents' house that had followed.

"Still," Pickett continued, "I would gladly suffer another cosh on the head if that would mean exchanging my traveling companion on that occasion for this one."

"Perhaps Harry Carson won't be so very bad," she said bracingly.

"Yes, and perhaps pigs will fly," he agreed.

She gave him a reproachful look, but said no more on the subject. All too soon, the abbreviated meal was finished, and there was no more reason to linger. With some reluctance, Pickett pushed back his chair and rose from the table. Julia followed, and hand in hand they made their way to the foyer. When they reached the front door, Pickett stopped, took her in his arms, and kissed her lingeringly.

"I wish I didn't have to go."

"The sooner you leave, the sooner you can return," she pointed out, although the arms she kept wrapped around his waist gave the lie to this encouraging farewell. "In the meantime, it gives you a little time to consider the matter before giving the prince your answer."

"Sweetheart, you will be careful, won't you?"

She smiled a little at the concern in his voice. "I think *I'm* supposed to be the one telling *you* that."

"And you have—many times. I promise to try, but I have to do my duty, even if it puts me in danger. But you—Julia, if you ever feel unsafe, or if anything just feels wrong, don't hesitate to go to Mr. Colquhoun. He and his wife will put you up for a few days if need be, until I come back."

Her eyes narrowed. "John, what is it that you think might happen?"

Pickett, realizing he was overplaying his hand rather badly, hastily demurred. "Nothing, really. It's just that I've never had to go off and leave you like this—not knowing how long I might have to be gone, I mean," he finished lamely, knowing she was remembering, as he was, the one time since their marriage that they had been apart for more than a few hours. On that occasion, they had parted in anger, and then spent the next thirty-six hours in abject misery.

Julia's arms tightened around him, and she laid her head against his chest. "Very well, then. If it will put your mind at ease so you may concentrate more fully on your investigations, I promise to go to Mr. Colquhoun at the first sign of trouble, real or imagined. Now, do I have your promise that you will do your best to return to me with a whole skin?"

"Believe me, I have every reason to come back to you in one piece."

"The prince," she agreed, nodding.

"No, *not* the prince," he retorted, dropping a kiss onto the golden curls tickling his chin. "Now, is there anything else I should do before I go?"

The question was strictly rhetorical, spoken more to himself than to her, but she took advantage of it nonetheless.

"You could always make me that proposal of marriage, you know."

He gave her a speaking look, but said, "I suppose I'd better be going, then. It looks like rain, and I have no desire to spend the next twelve hours sitting on the roof of the stagecoach."

"What an excellent way to change the subject," she said approvingly, and lifted her face for another kiss.

Pickett was nothing loth, and all too soon it was time to release her and step outside, where Thomas waited with his own bag as well as Pickett's.

He gave Thomas a smile and tried to act happier than he felt. "Well, Thomas, are you ready?"

* * *

Julia stood on the front stoop, watching them go—watching *him* go—and mentally chiding herself. What sort of wife was she? He'd been offered the opportunity of a lifetime, and she seemed determined to subtly turn him against it. *If you found this house overwhelming, only wait until you see the grand staircase at Carlton House*, she'd told him upon first hearing the news, knowing full well of the feelings of inadequacy that, she suspected, still plagued him on occasion. She hadn't even given him a proper goodbye without inserting the Prince of Wales into the conversation, implying that he was being asked to choose between them.

And then, when he'd refused to take the bait, she'd badgered him about making a wholly unnecessary gesture for no greater reason than the sentimental pleasure of seeing him go down on one knee. It was not as if she'd never received a marriage proposal at all; Frederick had uttered all the flowery phrases any romantically-minded young lady could ask for, and only look how *that* had turned out. No, she and John had something deeper, something that went beyond mere words; why, then, did she insist on hearing those words, when one of the qualities she found the most endearing in him was his tendency to become somewhat inarticulate whenever he spoke of his love for her? What sort of woman *wanted* to put her husband at a disadvantage?

As if he'd read her thoughts from a distance, he turned back and raised a hand in farewell. In answer, she pressed her fingers to her lips and blew him a kiss, silently vowing to remove to Carlton House with all the eagerness he might wish, if only he would come home safely. She watched until he disappeared from view, then stepped inside, closed the door, and climbed the stairs to her room and her empty bed.

* * *

In the meantime, Thomas had hefted his own bag with his left hand and Pickett's somewhat heavier bag with his stronger right, politely but firmly rebuffing Pickett's offers to carry his own bag as he cheerfully speculated on what sights they might expect to see on the road. Pickett listened to him with only half an ear, knowing from experience that most of the valet's expectations would die of sheer boredom after a few hours on the road. When they reached the point where Curzon Street intersected with Chapel West, he glanced back for one last look. Julia still stood on the front stoop, a small, pale figure in the gray dawn light. He lifted one hand in farewell, and when she put her hand to her face and blew him a kiss, it was only through a strong sense of duty and sheer force of will that he resisted the urge to turn around and go straight back to her, leaving Thomas standing on the street corner with the two bags he was determined to carry.

The quiet residential streets of Mayfair still slept, but by the time they reached Piccadilly, the darkness had lessened and the more commercial sections of London were stirring to life in spite of the rain that had indeed begun to fall. The vehicle that would convey them to Reading stood in the yard of the coaching house, the four stout horses stirring restlessly in their harnesses. Pickett, feeling something of the same impatience, suspected they wouldn't be nearly so eager once they were actually on the road. As for the driver, he was overseeing the several underlings who fastened onto the boot various valises, bandboxes, baskets, and even a crate containing live chickens. Clearly, they would have plenty of traveling companions on the journey. Pickett instructed Thomas to leave their bags with the driver, and then the two young men went inside, where Pickett handed their tickets to the booking agent and glanced about the room at the others waiting to board the coach. He was displeased, though hardly surprised, to find no sign of Harry Carson.

"If he's not here by the time we're allowed to board, we're going ahead without him," Pickett told Thomas. "I have no intention of sitting on the roof in the rain, all because Harry Carson can't get his carcass to the coaching house in time for us to get an inside seat."

"I'll sit up top," Thomas offered. "I don't mind."

"I won't let you get a wetting because of Harry—er, Mr.

Carson's tardiness," said Pickett, hastily reverting to the title by which Thomas would be expected to address his master's colleague.

"It's still a few minutes yet," Thomas said doubtfully, glancing up at the big clock. "Maybe he'll—"

"Sorry I'm late," a breathless voice interrupted.

Pickett, turning toward the sound, thought Harry didn't look very repentant. In fact, "smug" might have been a better description. He'd exchanged the blue coat and red waistcoat of the Bow Street Horse Patrol for a rather gaudy tailcoat of mustard-colored wool with wide lapels and a double row of large gold buttons—Pickett would have bet his entire week's wages that they were really pinchbeck—worn over a blue waistcoat made of what Pickett suspected was some of the cheaper silk produced in Spitalfields. Although these showy garments bore every appearance of having been donned in a hurry, the smile on Harry's handsome face could only be described as self-satisfied.

"What took you so long?" Pickett asked, making no attempt to mask his displeasure.

Harry Carson shrugged. "Couldn't disappoint a lady, could I?"

Yes, Pickett thought, *definitely self-satisfied.*

"Not that she's a lady in the same sense as your wife," Harry continued, "but—well, we can't all have viscountesses."

"You're out of uniform," Pickett said, uncomfortably aware of his own workaday brown serge and how it appeared next to Harry's more colorful ensemble. The contrast, along with the fact that he was by some few years the younger of the two, would have led any casual observer to deduce that Pickett was there to assist Carson, rather than the other way 'round.

"I'm supposed to be taking the place of a Runner, aren't I? You lot don't wear uniforms, so why should I?" Seeing that Pickett was not convinced, he added with a disarming grin, "If you're worrying about what the boss might say about it, well, I won't tell if you won't."

Determinedly ignoring the suggestion that he might deliberately mislead his magistrate, Pickett turned to Thomas. "Thomas, this is Mr. Carson of the Bow Street Horse Patrol. Harry, meet Thomas, my—my valet," he mumbled self-consciously.

"Pleased to meet you, sir," said Thomas, obviously much impressed with Carson's attire.

If Harry was aware of Pickett's *faux pas* in presenting him to Thomas, he didn't show it. Instead, his blue eyes widened. "Your *valet?* You travel with *servants* these days?"

"Not usually," Pickett said hastily. "But I've been putting Thomas off for too long already, and—"

"This ought to be fun!" Carson said, his grin widening. "'Thomas, my good fellow, go fetch me a cup of tea.' 'Thomas, shine my shoes.' 'Thomas—' "

"You're not to be ordering my valet about like he's your personal drudge," Pickett interrupted, halting Thomas in mid-step just as that conscientious young man was about to go in search of the requested cup of tea. Just to prove a point, he turned to his valet. "Thomas, go outside and find out how long it will be before we're able to board. Reserve three seats inside, if they'll let you."

"I don't mind sitting on the roof, sir," Thomas offered, unwilling to be the cause of any dissension.

"You're not going to sit on the roof! You're going to sit inside, and you're going to sit next to the window, so you have a good view."

"Yes, sir!" said Thomas, much gratified.

As it happened, Thomas was spared the necessity of carrying out this duty, as a general stirring in the room indicated that it was time to board the stagecoaches for the journey. They were fortunate enough to secure three seats inside, and Pickett, true to his word, made certain that Thomas was seated in the window; he'd put off his valet far too long not to make sure he got the most out of the long-awaited journey. Unfortunately, this seating arrangement had the unhappy effect of leaving Pickett with no more pleasurable alternative than that of making desultory conversation with Harry Carson.

"So," Harry began, after they had crossed the river Thames, and Newington and its environs had given way to open country, "how did you do it?"

"How did I do what?" Pickett asked, fearing the worst.

Harry shifted impatiently in his seat. "How did you marry a viscountess?"

Pickett, having no intention of recounting for Harry's edification the events that had led to his marriage, merely shrugged. "Just lucky, I guess."

"Dixon said you kept her from hanging for her husband's murder. Is that so?"

It was—at least, as far as it went—so Pickett nodded. "Yes."

Harry let out a long, low whistle. "Wish *I* could get promoted to principal officer. You fellows have all the luck."

Pickett might have pointed out several events in his career for which "luck" would have been a very peculiar description, but at that moment Thomas, having caught his first glimpse of an oast house, nudged his master and pointed at this curious structure, demanding to know what it was.

In such a manner the miles slowly passed. Pickett, his protracted farewells to his lady the previous night having left very little time for sleep, leaned his head back against the wall of the stagecoach and tried to make up for the deficit.

In this he was only partially successful, awaking at one point to hear Carson recounting to an enthralled Thomas, " . . . so there I was, facing three of them down, each one with two barkers apiece, and me with nothing more than a cutlass . . ."

"What did you do?" Thomas demanded breathlessly.

"He served the summons like he was supposed to, and then reported back to Bow Street," Pickett finished without opening his eyes.

"Much you know about it!" retorted Carson, perhaps justifiably goaded at having had his thunder stolen at the dramatic peak of his narrative.

Pickett opened his eyes. "I should think I do, considering that I did the work myself for almost five years." Turning to Thomas, he explained, "I'm afraid it isn't nearly as exciting as Mr. Carson makes it sound. In fact, any investigation is nine parts tedium."

"And the tenth part is apparently ingratiating oneself with wealthy widows," added Carson, with a sly look at Pickett.

"Better than ingratiating oneself with horses," Pickett replied. "I never envied you fellows on the Horse Patrol."

"You're on the Horse Patrol, then?" Thomas asked Carson.

Carson, having discovered that here was a topic into which his colleague could not follow, nodded. "My father owns a livery stable in Cheapside, so I've been around horses all my life. He hoped I would take over the business one day. It makes a tidy living for him and Mum and my sisters, but it always seemed like deadly dull work to me. I wanted more excitement, so I asked Lord Grantham—he sometimes rents a hack from my father when he's in Town—to recommend me to Bow Street. And he did," he concluded proudly, "so here I am. Still, it's not quite as exciting as I'd thought it would be, so I hope to be promoted to principal officer someday, like Mr. Pickett here."

Pickett examined this speech for some hidden insult, and found none. In fact, Harry Carson's account sounded strangely familiar: Even though his work hauling coal for Elias Granger had given him food in his belly and a roof over his head, he'd been aware of a craving for something more, something he could not have named, but which he'd looked for first in the books in Mr. Granger's library, and then in the fetching form of Mr. Granger's nubile daughter. Something he had eventually found, not in the position of a Bow Street principal officer, but in the arms of his lady wife. Perhaps, he conceded, he and Carson were more alike than he'd realized.

This charitable thought lasted until that evening in Reading. Having obtained a room at the White Hart for themselves and a place in the stables for Thomas, the three young men refreshed themselves with a hearty but plain meal of roast beef and potatoes before seeking their separate quarters for the night.

"Shall I come up for your boots, sir?" Thomas offered.

Pickett glanced down at his feet and discovered that his boots were indeed the worse for having traveled forty miles over dusty roads, even in an enclosed carriage. "Yes, thank you."

The valet turned uncertainly toward their traveling companion. "And Mr. Carson?"

Pickett nodded. "If you would be so good, Thomas, I would be obliged to you."

Upstairs in their room, they surrendered their footwear to Thomas, who bore them off for cleaning before seeking his own bed.

"You'll need to give him vails," Pickett advised Carson after they were alone.

Harry Carson looked bewildered. "I'll need to give him what?"

"Vails. Money. To show your appreciation for his services."

Carson was less than pleased with these instructions. "All very well and good if you're married to a wealthy woman, but for the rest of us—"

"It needn't be much, just a little something in recognition

of the fact that you're asking something of him that goes beyond his usual duties." Seeing that his colleague was inclined to be skeptical, he added, "Trust me on this, Carson. Of course, if you can't bring yourself to do so, I can always tell Thomas he needn't put himself out for you."

"Oh, all right, then." Carson turned away and began stripping off his coat and waistcoat, muttering something under his breath, the only discernable word of which was "hoity-toity."

Pickett, having made his point, shed his own coat, waistcoat, breeches, and stockings, and climbed between the sheets still clad in his shirt and drawers. These garments, which he found superfluous while in his own bed in Curzon Street, were preferable to bare skin against a mattress on which countless travelers would have slept before him—a mattress, which, to judge by the crackling sound that accompanied his every move, was stuffed with pea-shuckings, or perhaps straw; in any case, something other than the soft feathers upon which Julia was no doubt at that minute reposing.

Julia . . .

Obeying a sudden impulse, Pickett scrambled out of bed and padded in his bare feet across to the small table positioned beneath the window. He groped for the flint and lit the tallow candle, then fetched the small notebook and pencil he always carried in the inside pocket of his coat. He tore out a sheet, sat down before the table, and began to write:

My dearest love, I hope this finds you—what? Safe? Healthy? Alive? He didn't want to frighten her to death—*I hope this finds you well,* he wrote at last. *This is to inform you of my safe arrival in Reading. If all goes well, I shall reach Dunbury by tomorrow evening.*

"What are you doing?" asked Carson, who had by this time staked his claim to the other half of the bed.

"Writing a letter to my wife," Pickett said without looking up from the task at hand.

Once there, he continued, putting pencil to paper once more, *I hope to make a summary end to this business, whatever it may prove to be, and return to you with all due speed. Until then I am, always and forever,*

Yours,

John Pickett

He folded the paper and sealed it with a drop of wax from the candle, then wrote her name and direction on the outside before snuffing the candle and padding back to the bed. Alas, Carson, having been granted this brief glimpse into his marriage, had apparently lost all interest in sleep.

"What's it like, then?" he asked.

"What's what like?" asked Pickett, shifting on the crackling mattress in search of a relatively comfortable position.

"Having a viscountess in your bed," Carson answered impatiently, as if the answer should have been obvious.

Heaven, thought Pickett. *Paradise. Everything I ever dreamed of, yet never dared to hope for.* On that thought, he drifted toward slumber, and had almost achieved it when Carson, apparently taking his silence for an answer, spoke again.

"She's older than you, isn't she?"

"Mm-hm." In fact, Julia was two years his senior, but there were far greater differences between them than mere date of birth.

"So, what's it like?" Carson asked again. "Do you have to beg her pardon before you—"

"Shut up, Harry," growled Pickett, and turned his face to the wall.

4

In Which John Pickett's Quarry
Proves to Be Surprisingly Elusive

After an indifferent night's sleep interrupted at intervals by Carson's sleeping assurances to various damsels named Molly, Sally, and Peg that she was the only girl for him, Pickett awoke to a light scratching at the door. Throwing back the counterpane, he rolled out of bed—noticing that at some point in the night Carson had chosen to take his half down the middle, a fact that went some way toward explaining his own unsatisfying slumber—and padded across the room to the door. He opened it to find Thomas standing in the corridor holding Pickett's cleaned and polished boots in one hand; Carson's footwear stood on the floor beside him, presumably placed there in order to free up one hand for knocking.

"Good morning, sir," he greeted his master with a cheerfulness Pickett found disgusting. "Here's your boots, and Mr. Carson's, too. The polish is not quite what I would wish, but—well, it was late, and the lighting not the best so—" He broke off with an apologetic shrug.

"Never mind, Thomas. I'm sure they'll be much worse before the day is over. Have you had breakfast yet? No? We'll all go down together, then. Go pack your things, and we'll meet you in the public room in five minutes."

"Five minutes?" groaned a sleepy voice from beneath the counterpane. "You expect me to be ready in *five minutes?*"

"No, I expect Thomas to be ready in five minutes. I expect you to be ready in two and a half. The stagecoach won't wait, and I'd like a minute in front of the mirror to shave, too."

Harry Carson threw back the counterpane and crawled out of bed, mumbling something, very likely curses, under his breath. Pickett wasn't surprised when he took fully four minutes out of the five, obliging Pickett himself to make a hasty job of shaving before scrambling into his clothes. By the time they came downstairs, they found Thomas already waiting.

"I took the liberty of ordering breakfast for the three of us," he said apologetically. "I hope I haven't overstepped, but I was afraid there wouldn't be time, not with the coach already in the yard."

"No, you did very well," Pickett assured him, much more in charity with his valet at the moment than he was with his colleague.

As Thomas had said, the stagecoach already stood before the door, and the public room was overflowing with passengers either fortifying themselves for the next stage of the journey or awaiting the signal to board. They made a hasty repast of porridge, washing it down with weak coffee before joining the throng picking their way across the muddy yard to the waiting carriage. Several of their fellow travelers had reached their destination in Reading, but their places were taken by new passengers, so the vehicle was no less full than it had been before.

Pickett, squeezed between Thomas and a stout man smelling of tobacco, recalled his first journey by stagecoach only the previous summer, when he had been summoned to Yorkshire. On that occasion, he hadn't been overly troubled by the crowded, poorly sprung carriage; he'd been eager to see something of the world beyond London. Or so he had told himself; in fact, he'd been even more eager to see Julia—or, rather, Lady Fieldhurst, as she was then. Since that time, he'd become accustomed to traveling by post-chaise. He supposed the Prince of Wales would have his own private carriage— very likely more than one—and wondered how His Royal Highness would expect his personal bodyguard to accompany him. *Please, God, not on horseback,* he prayed silently. He was resolved to do whatever it took to return Julia to something approaching her rightful place in society, but there were some sacrifices he would prefer not to have to make.

Their progress was slower today, for the rain had steadily increased since they'd left London. The windows of the stagecoach were spotted with raindrops which ran down the glass and mingled with the mud thrown up onto the panes by the horses' hooves, leaving Pickett with no more pleasant way to pass the time than listening with barely concealed impatience as Harry Carson regaled Thomas with a highly embellished account of his career with the Bow Street Horse Patrol, including a number of occasions on which he'd got his man only through great cunning and physical courage. The knowledge that he himself might have held Thomas equally enrapt at any time over the past six months, had he been inclined to boast of his own exploits, made Carson's tales no easier to stomach, and the fact that most of their fellow passengers had abandoned their own attempted amusements in order to listen admiringly to the supposed hero in their midst made them more intolerable still. It was not until Harry turned his attention to Thomas, however, that Pickett was moved to protest.

"You seem like an intelligent fellow," Carson told Thomas, who visibly preened at this praise. "Maybe you should consider going to work for Bow Street yourself."

"I don't know—" Thomas demurred modestly.

"Are you trying to steal my valet?" demanded Pickett.

Carson, seated directly opposite Thomas, turned his attention to Pickett. "You can't blame a man for being ambitious. Maybe Thomas here wants something more out of life than starching your cravats and polishing your boots."

"Well—" Thomas began feebly.

"You *are* trying to steal my valet!"

The tobacco-scented man made a shooing motion with his hands. "Never mind that!"

"Get on with the story," the farm wife seated next to Harry urged impatiently.

Harry was nothing loth, and Pickett, clearly in the

minority, lapsed into surly silence.

Even the most tedious of journeys must eventually come to an end, and Pickett breathed a sigh of relief as the stagecoach lurched into the yard of the Cock and Boar and rolled to a stop. The passengers disembarked slowly in spite of the rain that still fell in sheets, the long hours of inactivity having rendered their muscles stiff and sore. In less inclement weather, Pickett might have gone inside to procure a room for the night, leaving Thomas to reclaim their bags from the boot. But as he had no doubt that Carson would follow him inside, leaving Thomas to fetch his bag as well, he remained resolutely outside in the rain until all three bags had been cut loose and tossed down, taking what satisfaction he could from the sight of rainwater dripping from the curled brim of Carson's hat.

Once all three valises had been returned to their respective owners, Pickett led the way inside and took his place in the throng of travelers procuring rooms, having either reached their destination or broken their journeys for the night before resuming the journey to Wells in the morning. As before, Thomas was given a place over the stables while Pickett and Carson were assigned a room upstairs, inside the inn proper.

Just before surrendering his place in line to the person behind him (whose enormous and no doubt muddy portmanteau was pressing against the backs of his legs), Pickett raised his voice to be heard above the crowd as he inquired of the innkeeper, "Can you tell me in which room I might find Mr. Edward Gaines Brockton? I'm supposed to meet him here."

With a distracted sigh, the innkeeper flipped back a page in his ledger. "Mr. Brockton is in the room right next to yours, at the top of the stairs."

"Thank you," Pickett said, and squeezed his way past the portmanteau and back to his traveling companions.

Together they climbed the stairs, Pickett feeling more than a little foolish at carrying nothing more burdensome than the key to the room while Carson followed with his own valise and Thomas brought up the rear with the bags of both master and servant. As they reached the top of the stairs, however, a dilemma presented itself. *Mr. Brockton is in the room right next to yours, at the top of the stairs,* the innkeeper had said. Had he meant that Mr. Brockton's room was at the top of the stairs, and theirs was the room just beyond it, or was it their own room that was at the top of the stairs?

He wished he had noticed the ambiguity of the statement before giving up his place in line, but it was too late now. Besides the fact that he would have to wait his turn all over again, he didn't want to give Harry Carson any evidence of incompetence with which to torment him. There was nothing for it but to insert the key into the lock of the first room at the top of the stairs, and pray that it opened. If not, he would make the acquaintance of Mr. Edward Gaines Brockton a bit earlier than anticipated, and under less felicitous circumstances than he might have wished. If that should prove to be the case, well, he would have to put Carson off with some nonsense about catching the fellow off his guard.

His mind made up, he inserted the key into the lock,

pushed the door open, and beheld the room that was to be his home for the foreseeable future. Granted, very little of the room was visible at the moment beyond vague shapes, as it was now fully dark outside and no fire had been lit in the grate in anticipation of the new arrivals. Still, Pickett was by this time well-traveled enough to know that most such rooms were very much alike. The large shape against the adjacent wall was the bed, which he would be obliged to share with Carson; the smaller shape next to it was the washstand, before which he and Carson would no doubt jockey for position in the morning; the low, square shape beneath the window was a writing table, where he would sit down and compose a brief letter to Julia, informing her of his safe arrival. Before he could settle down to this domestic task, however, there were certain things that had to be done.

"Choose your side, Harry, and I'll take the other," he told Carson, gesturing toward the bed. "Thomas, if you'll get the fire started, I'll go next door and introduce myself to Mr. Brockton. I doubt he'll want to open his budget just yet, not with such a din downstairs, but perhaps it will save us some time in the morning."

Carson needed no urging. He sat down on the edge of the bed nearest the window, dropping his valise at his feet with the air of an explorer planting a flag. Meanwhile, Thomas knelt before the cold grate and groped about in the darkness for the flint.

As for Pickett, he left the room, walked the few feet down the corridor to the next door, and rapped upon it. Receiving no answer, he tried again, this time calling, "Mr.

Brockton? Mr. Brockton, it's John Pickett, from Bow Street."

Still no answer. Either Mr. Brockton had gone out and not returned, or else he had already sought his bed—in which case he would not be pleased to be roused in his nightshirt by a travel-stained fellow whose companions were apparently dismantling their room board by board, if the noise they were making was anything to judge by. It appeared Pickett would be obliged to wait until morning after all. Giving up a lost cause, he returned to his room, consoling himself with the realization that, if Mr. Brockton had indeed gone out, he would almost certainly hear the man return, given the seeming thinness of the walls.

"What the devil is going on in here?" Pickett asked irritably as he re-entered his own room.

The answer to his question was self-evident. The fire had been lit, and Thomas was now engaged in emptying Pickett's valise into the clothes-press provided for that purpose. As they had not unpacked their bags the previous night—given that they would be back on the road at first light, it had seemed an unnecessary waste of time—this was Harry Carson's first look at Pickett's clothing beyond the brown serge coat he usually wore to Bow Street, which he had also worn on the stagecoach.

"I say, you've come up in the world!" Carson exclaimed. He snatched a dark blue double-breasted tailcoat out of Thomas's hands and held it up to his own chest. "I didn't know you planned to make your bow to the Prince of Wales on this trip."

Actually, Carson was closer to the truth than he knew,

but Pickett wasn't about to make him a gift of this information; he would never hear the end of it. "My wife's parents live not far from here," he said, albeit not without reluctance. "If I have time, I might have to pay Sir Thaddeus and Lady Runyon a visit while I'm in the area."

" 'Sir' Thaddeus! 'Lady' Runyon! Lord, but you're moving in rarified circles these days!" Carson slid his arms into the sleeves of Pickett's evening coat and examined the results in the mirror over the washstand. "Look! The sleeves come all the way down over my hands! It's a pity you're such a long-shanks, for I wouldn't half mind borrowing this."

"I wouldn't let you, even if it fit," Pickett informed him. "Now, if you'll let Thomas put my clothes away, I need to write a letter to my wife."

Carson grinned knowingly. "What, another one? Keeps you on a short leash, doesn't she?"

"The shortest," Pickett agreed, with a secretive smile of his own. And so she did, although not quite in the way Harry meant. No, the tie that bound him to Julia was one of love, not obligation, and certainly not financial dependence, although that was of necessity one aspect of their unequal marriage.

Thomas had lit the lamp on the writing table, so Pickett sat down, tore another page from his notebook, and began to compose his letter.

My dearest love,

This is to inform you that I reached Dunbury safely just after sunset. I have discovered which room belongs to my quarry, but as there was no answer to my knock, I must assume that he has gone out, and my questions to him must wait until tomorrow. In the meantime, the worst has happened: Harry Carson has discovered my clothes, and as I write these words, he is peacocking about the room in the blue coat which I will always associate with the day we were wed.

Actually, this was not the worst that could happen—far from it, in fact—but Julia was happy in the mistaken belief that he had put the events of the Lake District behind him, and he had no desire to disabuse her of this comfortable, if erroneous, notion. He supposed he might, someday, but not until he was certain the business was unequivocally concluded. In the meantime, he would have the satisfaction of knowing, even across the miles that separated them, that he had made her laugh.

It is fortunate for me that I am fully half a head taller than he, he continued, *or I would very likely have nothing left to me but the shirt on my back. Thomas, unlike his master, is having the time of his life. Although I could wish he were not quite so inclined to hero-worship where Carson is concerned, Carson having whiled away the miles by recounting his heroic deeds on the Horse Patrol, fully half of which I suspect took place only in his imagination. I shall seek clarification on this point from Mr. Colquhoun upon my return, which cannot come soon enough. Until that day I am, always and forever,*

Yours,

John

Having finished this missive, Pickett folded it and directed it to Mrs. John Pickett at 22 Curzon Street in London, then dripped melting wax from the candle on it to seal it against prying eyes—Harry Carson's mocking blue ones came to mind—before dismissing Thomas to his own lodgings above the stables.

"So, what do we do next, chief?" asked Harry. He had surrendered Pickett's coat to Thomas, and now stood regarding his superior in nothing but his shirtsleeves.

"We make an early night of it, and start fresh in the morning," Pickett said with a sigh.

In fact, he fully intended to lie in bed listening for the return of the man in the next room. If he was lucky, Mr. Brockton would return before the hour grew too late, and Pickett could slip his clothes back on, go next door, and have a word with the fellow without the added distractions of Carson and Thomas. Alas, he had failed to reckon on the cumulative effects of two nights of very little slumber. His head had hardly hit the pillow before he was fast asleep. And although on this night Carson's muttered endearments were reserved for a girl named Betty, Pickett never heard them.

* * *

Pickett awoke much refreshed the following morning, and lingered in the room only long enough to wash, shave, and dress before betaking himself down the corridor to the room next door. Once again, he rapped sharply upon the door, and waited. No one opened the door to him, nor did he hear any sounds coming from within the room. Pickett stifled any qualms about rousing the man from sleep; if one went to the trouble of summoning a Runner—two, in fact—from London, one might jolly well get out of bed and talk to him. Steeling his resolve, he knocked again, harder this time, and put his ear to the wooden panel.

The chamber within was silent; the term "silent as the grave" rose unbidden to Pickett's mind. Was it possible that Mr. Brockton had died at some point during the night—perhaps by natural causes, perhaps not—while he lay sleeping only a few feet away? If that should prove to be the case, then he would knock in vain. It might be days before the death was discovered, and in the meantime the murderer—if murderer there were—would have plenty of time to escape the scene of the crime.

Cautioning himself against leaping to conclusions, Pickett descended the stairs. A pretty young woman in an apron and mobcap now held the place occupied last night by the innkeeper; his daughter, Pickett supposed.

"Excuse me," he told the girl, "I should like a word with Mr. Brockton, the fellow in the room next to mine, but he doesn't answer my knock. Do you happen to know if he's gone out?"

She looked up at him with wide eyes of cornflower blue, and tucked a blonde curl back into her cap. "Why, I expect he's gone to divine services."

So firmly had the idea of Brockton's murder taken hold of Pickett's brain that her speculations brought to mind the image of funerals. "Divine—?"

"It's Sunday," she reminded him. "I expect he's at church."

"Oh—oh yes, of course. Thank you," Pickett said, shaking his head as if to clear it. It was a curious consequence of travel that one tended to lose track of time, as if both clock and calendar ceased to function while one was enclosed in a carriage. On the other hand, the fact that it was Sunday might actually make it easier to run his quarry to earth; as shops were closed, entertainments were few, and travel was discouraged—if not impossible, since neither the stage nor the mail coaches ran on Sunday—there was little Mr. Brockton could do but take walks or cool his heels in his room. Pickett considered these possibilities as he climbed the stairs to the room and opened the door. Seeing Carson still abed, he crossed the room in three strides and flung back the bedclothes.

"Get up, Harry," he said, not without a certain satisfaction. "We're going to church. If half the things you mutter in your sleep are true, you need it."

5

In Which John Pickett and His Magistrate
Seek Spiritual Guidance

A t his home in Mayfair, magistrate Patrick Colquhoun
stood before the mirror tying his cravat. While in his
native country, and as a very young man in the American
colony of Virginia, Mr. Colquhoun had been as Presbyterian
as any good lowland Scot; being a pragmatic man, however,
he had attended the parish church of St. George's Hanover
Square since settling in London almost a quarter-century ago,
and it was in preparation for services there that he now
scowled fiercely at his reflection, and at the unsatisfactory
strip of starched linen encircling his throat. He had never
aspired to the dandy set, however, so instead of beginning
again with a fresh neckcloth, he began to coax the folds into a
more acceptable form. He had almost achieved this modest
goal when he was interrupted by a knock at the front door of
the town house.

"Oh, the devil," he grumbled, for it was the servants' day

off. The task of answering the door would fall to the master of the house.

"Never mind, dear, I'll get it," called his wife, Janet, who had finished her own toilette and was awaiting him in the drawing room downstairs.

She joined him in the bedroom a few minutes later with a folded square of paper in her hand and a thoughtful frown on her brow.

"A courier just brought this," she said, surrendering the missive to her husband. "I hope it isn't bad news."

Mr. Colquhoun took the paper, broke the seal, and opened the fold. He scanned the brief message, and gave utterance to a few choice words wholly inappropriate for a man on his way to divine services.

"I expect it must be important, for him to be delivering it on Sunday," Janet Colquhoun hinted broadly.

She might have saved her breath.

"Is the courier still here?" he asked sharply.

"Why, no! I felt sorry for the poor fellow, being obliged to work on the Sabbath, so I gave him a half a crown for his trouble and sent him on his way."

The last part of this speech fell on deaf ears. Mr. Colquhoun, his cravat forgotten, hastily exited the room, then ran down the stairs, flung open the door, and stepped out onto the portico, looking left and right. The courier was long gone.

"You weren't able to catch him, I suppose," Mrs. Colquhoun remarked sympathetically when her husband rejoined her in the bedroom.

He shook his head in answer, but she had the distinct

impression that his mind was already somewhere else. "No, but I daresay it's just as well. There's nothing the lad could do, even if he were here, and there's no sense in summoning him all the way from—" He broke off, looking at his wife as if seeing her for the first time. "Are you ready, Janet? Let's be off to church, then. I feel a sudden urge to pray."

* * *

Harry Carson, on the other hand, was considerably less enthusiastic as he and Pickett traversed the short distance from the inn to the fourteenth-century stone church that served the residents of Dunbury and its environs. Nor was he shy about letting his displeasure be known.

"And what's more," he said, continuing his catalog of grievances as they passed through the lych-gate and into the churchyard, "I don't see why I have to wear my work clothes." He cast a contemptuous glance down at his person, clad in the blue coat and red waistcoat of the Bow Street Horse Patrol. "After all, this fellow—Brockton, did you say?—he asked for two Runners, and you fellows aren't in uniform."

"No," Pickett conceded, "but half the general public doesn't seem to recognize that. If he's looking for us, I want him to have no trouble in picking us out. Look at it this way," he said, making an appeal to Carson's vanity, which he knew to be robust, "If this Mr. Brockton is at church, as the innkeeper's daughter seems to think he must be, he'll very likely take one look at you and recognize you as one of the Runners he sent for."

"You think so?" Harry's expression lightened somewhat before descending once more into gloom. "That is, he might think so, until he makes our acquaintance—at which point you will no doubt enlighten him as to which of us is the superior."

"Well, yes," agreed Pickett, unrepentant. "After all, he asked for me by name."

"Exactly! Then why is it *our* job to seek *him* out? Seems to me the shoe ought to be on the other foot."

A shadow crossed Pickett's face. "Remember, we don't yet know why he wanted us. If he's in any danger, if someone else gets to him first—" He broke off, shaking his head. *This is not the Lake District,* he reminded himself. *What happened there has no bearing on whatever it is we're supposed to be doing here.*

On that occasion, someone had indeed murdered his contact before Pickett could discover why he'd been sent for, forcing him to construct the case piecemeal. In the end, he had barely escaped with his life, but not before causing, however unintentionally, the death of an innocent woman. He still dreamed of it some nights, dreamed that he was once again holding the pistol, only this time he tried in vain to point it somewhere else, to aim it in any direction except toward the woman standing in the open doorway. The result was always the same. The gun went off, the woman fell, and when he knelt and turned the body over, it was Julia, his own wife, who lay there, bright red blood spreading across the bodice of her white gown. At that point he would awaken to find the sheets beneath him soaked through with perspiration.

Harry Carson had never been accused of being especially perceptive—not even by his friends—but something in Pickett's expression told its own tale, or perhaps he remembered hearing something at Bow Street. In any case, he nodded, said, "Whatever you say, chief," and followed Pickett into the church without further protest.

Even with Harry's cooperation, however, Pickett's plan left much to be desired. He'd assumed that, since Mr. Brockton was putting up at the inn, he must be a stranger to the area, or at least no longer resided there, and thought the church-going citizens of Dunbury might betray some curiosity toward a stranger in their midst. And this assumption was correct, so far as it went; unfortunately, the only curiosity displayed by the locals was aimed at two handsome young men in their midst, one a tall young man with curling brown hair and an air of reserve, the other a golden-haired Adonis clad in the blue coat and red waistcoat of London's famed Bow Street men.

After taking a seat in one of the pews, Pickett was disconcerted to scan the faces of the congregation only to discover that a large portion of them were looking back in his direction. Knowing his colleague's reputation with the fair sex (and had he not already been aware of this, Carson's nocturnal mutterings would have been more than sufficient to educate him on the subject), Pickett was not surprised that most of these curious glances came from females with more than a passing interest in Harry's *beaux yeux*. He made a mental note to remind Carson of his duty, and suffered a check when his gaze met that of a beautiful titian-haired woman in her mid-thirties, a woman whose black gown and bonnet denoted the recent widow. So taken aback was he by the lady's obvious interest that his eyebrows rose of their own accord. The lady clearly interpreted this gesture as a question—"Me?"—for in answer she gave an infinitesimal nod. Pickett, feeling the heat rise to his face, fixed his gaze upon the elderly vicar in the pulpit, and kept it there.

At the end of the service, Pickett and Carson joined the throng moving toward the door. As the vicar was stationed there, shaking hands and exchanging greetings with the various members of his flock, their progress was of necessity slow. Pickett, uncomfortably aware of the curious gazes that followed them, accepted the vicar's proffered handshake with a sense of profound relief.

"Welcome, welcome!" the vicar said warmly. "So pleased you could join us today. Tell me, are you new to the area? I don't recall having met you before. But then, my memory is not what it was, so one never knows . . ." He broke off with a shake of his head.

"No, sir, we've never met," Pickett said. "I'm John Pickett, and this is my colleague, Harry Carson. We just arrived yesterday from London."

"From London, is it?" He turned to offer his hand to Harry, and his myopic gaze sharpened at the sight of the well-known red waistcoat. "Would you be from Bow Street, by any chance?"

It was Pickett who answered for both of them. "As a matter of fact, yes." Carson's uniform might have provided the opening, just as Pickett had hoped it might, but he was not about to let the fellow forget which one of them was in charge of the investigation. "We were summoned to Dunbury to meet with a man called Brockton. He's supposedly staying at the same inn—we're putting up at the Cock and Boar—but so far our luck has been out. The innkeeper's daughter seemed to think he might have gone to church this morning, so we came in the hope of making contact with him."

The vicar stroked his receding chin thoughtfully. "Dear me, I don't—Brockton, you say?"

Pickett nodded. "Edward Gaines Brockton, to be exact."

"I'm afraid I've never met the man. And I fear Dunbury is not so large as to allow strangers to pass unnoticed—as you are no doubt aware, having been the objects of considerable curiosity yourselves."

As if on cue, the flame-haired widow came swanning up to take the vicar's hand, although Pickett would have sworn that she hadn't been standing behind them in the line. "Such an uplifting sermon! I wouldn't have missed it for worlds!" She cast an appraising glance over her shoulder at Pickett. "But who are your friends, Vicar? I don't believe I've had the pleasure."

Apparently the vicar's mind was so affixed on higher things that the urges of the flesh were unknown to him, or else he was well enough acquainted with the widow that her forwardness did not shock him. Either way, he seemed to take the question at face value. "Ah, good morning, Mrs. Avery. This is Mr. Pickett and his colleague, Mr. Carson. Mr. Pickett, Mr. Carson, allow me to present Mrs. Avery, one of my most charming parishioners. Mrs. Avery, these men have come from London in search of a Mr. Brockton. I don't suppose you know of such a man?"

Pickett did not wonder that the vicar should ask her such

a question; he suspected there were few men in the district whom the widow did *not* know.

"Brockton, Brockton," echoed the widow, her ivory brow puckered in a thoughtful frown. "The name is somewhat familiar, but I don't—oh, wait!"

"You've thought of something?" asked the vicar.

"I believe so. But we must not keep you waiting, for I'm sure there must be dozens of people who wish to speak to you. I shall bid you good day, Vicar, and surrender my place to another."

And so saying, she slipped her black-gloved hand into Pickett's arm and bore him off, scarcely leaving him time to make his own farewells to the vicar, much less thank him for his assistance. Carson, Pickett noticed, had apparently drawn his own conclusions regarding the widow's interest in the case, for instead of accompanying them as they crossed the churchyard, he abandoned them in favor of his own pursuits, most of which appeared to be centered on a bucolic beauty wearing a gypsy hat tied with pink ribbons over her ebony curls. Pickett would have liked to remonstrate with him regarding his duty, but as his own duty consisted of discovering what the widow might know of the elusive Mr. Brockton, he was obliged to delay any such action until they had returned to the Cock and Boar. In the meantime, Pickett and the widow had almost reached the lych-gate, and she had not yet spoken a word on the subject.

"We were speaking of Mr. Brockton," he reminded her. "What can you tell me about him?"

She glanced about the churchyard. "I don't like to speak

here. One never knows who might be listening."

Pickett followed her gaze, and found that the churchyard was rapidly emptying as the vicar's congregation dispersed to their homes. The vicar still stood in the doorway, nodding as he listened to a lengthy monologue from an elderly lady, and Harry had transferred his fickle attentions to a flaxen-haired damsel in a print dress, but aside from these few, Pickett and Mrs. Avery were very nearly alone.

"Yes, it is no doubt foolish of me," she added quickly, apparently discerning his thoughts, "but—well, when one lives alone, one tends to fall prey to any number of fanciful notions! When Avery was alive, I never—but I shall not bore you with all that! My house is the last but one in the High Street, just past the bookseller's shop. Do say you will join me for tea tomorrow! I believe I can make it worth your while."

"Why tomorrow?" Pickett asked, unable to completely repress the hint of impatience that crept into his voice at the thought of yet another delay.

"Not here," she said again, shaking her head emphatically. "When one is a widow, people are inclined to talk."

For his part, Pickett thought people would be much more inclined to gossip about a widow entertaining a man privately in her home than they would about a conversation that took place in the churchyard within full view of anyone who cared to look. But then the widow demurely lowered her head. With her face hidden from his view, Pickett was forcibly reminded of another young widow clad in the unrelieved black of mourning, and the way her so-called "friends" had turned on her in the days following her husband's murder.

"Very well," he found himself saying. "What time do you want me?"

6

*In Which Are Seen Two Opposing Methods
of Investigative Work*

I f *you* can have an assignation, I don't see why *I* can't have one," Harry grumbled as they made their way back to the Cock and Boar.

"It's not an assignation," Pickett insisted, not for the first time.

Harry gave a snort of derision. "You may say that, but I'll wager the Widow Avery has her own ideas on the subject! If she wanted to talk to you privately, why didn't she do it there in the churchyard? There was no one else to hear."

Pickett had thought the same thing, but now he found himself compelled to defend the widow's actions—or, perhaps, his own acceptance of the lady's invitation. "She was right when she said people are prone to talk. Widows are sometimes held to a different standard from other women."

Something in his expression must have given him away, for Harry regarded him with a knowing look. "And you—or rather, your wife—should know, eh?"

They had reached the inn by this time, and so Pickett was spared the necessity of making an answer. He stopped before the counter that served as both bar and registration desk, and the innkeeper's daughter brightened at their appearance, although the coy glances she cast toward some point beyond Pickett's shoulder gave him to understand that it was not he who brought the blush to her cheeks.

"Tell me, have you seen Mr. Brockton come in?" he asked.

"Why, no, sir," she said, shifting her attention from one young man to the other. "He wasn't at church, then?"

"Apparently not."

The girl expressed her disappointment that her suggestion hadn't been more helpful, but could offer no further assistance. Pickett placed a silver shilling on the counter and slid it across to her.

"I would be obliged to you if you'll let us know when you see him come in," he said. "You might let him know, too, that we've been asking for him."

She snatched up the coin eagerly, promising that when Mr. Brockton put in an appearance, Pickett and his colleague would be the first to know. With this he was forced to be content, but at the top of the stairs he turned to Harry.

"You can go on to our room. I'm going to have one more try at bearding the lion in his den."

Harry readily agreed, and a moment later Pickett was knocking once more on the door next to theirs. Once again, there was no answer.

"I don't suppose our man could be a Nonconformist," Pickett speculated without much conviction as he joined Harry in their room. "I believe some of those Methodist sermons can run rather long."

"Don't tell me you're going to drag me off to some other church next Sunday!" exclaimed Harry, who had already shed his blue coat and was in the process of unbuttoning his red waistcoat.

"No, for by next Sunday I hope to be back in London," Pickett said emphatically.

Harry regarded him with a quizzical expression. "You sound awfully sure of yourself. Do you have such high hopes for the widow, then?"

Pickett let out a long sigh. "Wishful thinking, I'm afraid. Until we can discover why Brockton sent for us, our hands are tied."

"Look here," Harry began haltingly, with none of the impudence that usually characterized his conversation, "do you suppose the fellow might be—I don't know—*unable* to meet with us?"

Pickett frowned. "Exactly what are you suggesting?"

Harry gave an uncomfortable little laugh. "I guess I'm wondering if he might be dead."

Pickett regarded his colleague with new respect. In fact, he had wondered that very thing—more than once, in fact, but his suspicions were influenced by the case he had worked a month earlier in the Lake District, in which his contact had been murdered before Pickett could discover the reason for his summons. He had not expected the same discernment from

Harry Carson, and acknowledged somewhat ruefully that, once again, Mr. Colquhoun knew what he was doing.

"Go ahead, tell me I'm barmy," Harry said with a nervous laugh, breaking the strained silence. "It won't be the first time I've heard it."

Pickett shook his head. "No, no, it isn't that. In fact, I've wondered the same thing. It's too soon to jump to any conclusions, but we must consider the possibility."

"So, what do we do now, chief? Comb the area for a body?"

"Not just yet. First we need to find someone—anyone!— who can tell us about Brockton."

"Exactly what is it that you want to know?"

Pickett sank onto the foot of the bed with another sigh, this one of frustration. "Anything would be an improvement. At this point, I'd settle for knowing what the fellow looks like."

"In that case, I'm your man," declared Harry, quite in his old manner.

"Oh? And how is that?"

"In case you hadn't noticed, that game pullet downstairs seems to fancy me."

"The innkeeper's daughter, you mean?"

"If there's another one, I hadn't noticed her. You take the Widow Avery; I'll take our host's daughter."

"I was thinking of starting out with the stables. Unless he came on the stage, Brockton must have left his rig, or else a hack, there. I shall have to inquire."

"Why not let Thomas do it?"

"What's that?" Pickett asked, with an arrested expression.

"Let Thomas do it," Harry said again.

"You're determined to steal my valet, aren't you?"

"Not at all," Harry assured him. "Thomas is putting up over the stables, so he's bound to have formed some connections there. They might talk more freely to him than they would to either of us." As Pickett pondered the practicality of this suggestion, Carson enlarged upon it. "Of course, if he finds that assisting in an investigation is more exciting than ironing your neckcloths—well, I can see why you might not want to tempt him."

"I'll have you know I trust Thomas implicitly!"

"Of course you do," Harry agreed. "Just not so much that you would let him take part in the investigation, when he's dying for a piece of it."

"Just not so much that I would put an amateur in a position where he might *literally* die for a piece if it," Pickett retorted. In a more moderate tone, he added, "You may never have been in a spot where your life was in danger, but I have. I would never intentionally put someone else in that position."

A more perceptive person than Harry Carson might have noticed Pickett's expression and deduced that he was no longer thinking of his valet. But at that moment there was a light scratching at the door, and it opened to reveal Thomas bearing an armload of wet linen.

"I've taken the liberty of washing your things, sir, and Mr. Carson's, too," he told Pickett. "Mind you, I wouldn't usually do such a thing on a Sunday, but I didn't know when else I might get dibs on the laundry room. I'm afraid I'll have to hang them in here to dry. I could do it in the stable, but I didn't think you'd want your shirts smelling like horse."

"No, thank you," Pickett said emphatically. "I'm sure we can tolerate being a bit crowded while they dry."

"I say, Thomas," Harry put in before Pickett could shush him, "you wouldn't mind asking a few questions around the stables, would you?"

Thomas brightened at once. "Me? You mean it, sir?"

As this last was directed toward Pickett, he was obliged perforce to agree. "We still haven't been able to run this Mr. Brockton to ground. Mr. Carson thought you might have formed some connections in the stables, and that they might be more likely to talk to you than they would to either of us."

"Well, I won't deny that me and a few of the lads got up a game of nine-pins after they'd fed and watered all the horses," Thomas admitted. "Still, I wouldn't want it to be known that I suspected them of anything havey-cavey."

"We don't suspect anyone of anything," Pickett put in quickly. "We just want to find someone who has seen the elusive Mr. Brockton."

"I'll see what I can find out, sir," Thomas declared stoutly.

"In the meantime, perhaps you could do something about this loose button," his master continued, displaying the one at the band of his left wrist and at the same time giving Thomas a subtle reminder of the real purpose for which he had been allowed to accompany Pickett on the journey.

Having dispatched Thomas on this errand and Carson to

see what he might discover from the innkeeper's beauteous daughter, Pickett spent a quiet afternoon in the room, listening for any sound that might suggest Mr. Brockton's presence in the room next door. Having nothing else to do with himself, he twice walked down the corridor and tried knocking on the door again, but with no more satisfactory results than he'd had before. He supposed he might write another letter to Julia, but he had very little to tell. He'd made no progress on the investigation at all beyond an assignation—there was that word again—with Mrs. Avery the next day, and he had no intention of divulging such a thing to his wife, lest she draw the same conclusions as Harry Carson had done. In fact, there was nothing he could say to her but *I'm very lonely* and *I miss you very much*—in other words, requiring her to pay a shilling only to be cast into a fit of the dismals.

He brightened somewhat when Thomas returned from his errand, but the valet's report was not encouraging.

"No one in the stables has seen hide nor hair of anyone named Brockton, although I asked 'em all," Thomas said.

"And none of the rigs in the stable belong to him? None of the hacks?"

Thomas's gaze faltered. "I couldn't say, sir. I didn't think to ask 'em that." Seeing that this was the wrong answer, he was eager to make amends. "I can go back down and ask, sir. I can be back in a trice—"

Pickett sighed. "Never mind, Thomas. That won't be necessary."

"I'm sorry sir," Thomas said, clearly feeling some further commentary was called for. "I didn't know—didn't think—"

"It's all right," Pickett assured him, and tried hard to mean it. "It's not your fault. It's mine, for sending you on such an errand without any preparation."

"Yes, sir," Thomas said, albeit with so hangdog an expression that Pickett felt compelled to offer some further consolation.

"Look, Thomas," he began haltingly, "you should know that this occupation is not nearly so exciting as Mr. Carson makes it sound. In fact, I should say any investigation is nine parts tedium. Still, if you're that interested in—that is, if you're no longer happy in service and have a mind to try something else, I would—I would be glad to speak to Mr. Colquhoun on your behalf."

The valet's eyes grew round. "You'd do that for me, sir?"

"If you wanted it, yes. You should be aware, though, that a man on the Foot Patrol earns quite a bit less than you're being paid as a valet. It's not until one is promoted to principal officer and can accept private commissions that one has the opportunity to earn real money."

"Yes, sir," Thomas said, nodding his head vigorously. "I understand."

"You should know, too, that I would dislike very much to lose you as a valet," Pickett confessed. "I don't know where I would find another one who wouldn't look down his nose at me as if I were something he'd discovered stuck to the bottom of his shoe."

"I'm sure anyone ought to consider himself lucky to have an employer as easy to please—"

The door flew open to admit Carson, breathing heavily

and stuffing the tail of his shirt into the waistband of his breeches with more regard for haste than fashion.

"Carson?" Pickett stared in bewilderment as his colleague slammed the door shut behind him and leaned against the panel as if to barricade it. "What the—?"

"Had to—get away—" Harry panted. "Escaped—out the window—"

At last, Pickett thought, *we seem to be getting somewhere!* Aloud, he asked, "Who was it, Carson? Who was after you?"

"Father," was Harry's breathless reply.

"Your father?" echoed Pickett, bewildered.

"Not mine—hers."

"Whose?" Pickett asked in growing impatience.

"Nancy—innkeeper's daughter."

Revelation dawned. "Devil take it, Harry, can't you question a possible witness with your breeches *up?*"

"Of course I can!" retorted Harry, bristling at this slur upon his investigative skills. "But why would I want to? Far more pleasant with 'em down, you know," he added with an impudent grin.

"We didn't come to Dunbury for your personal enjoyment! Did you manage to discover anything useful, or were you too busy er—um—" Pickett's attempt at a stern reproof was considerably hampered by his inability to come up with a suitable word for his colleague's actions that was not insulting to Nancy, however obliging that damsel might have been.

Harry, recognizing Pickett's dilemma, did nothing to

help him, but observed his struggles with wicked amusement.

Seeing no assistance was to be had from that quarter, Pickett returned to his original question, this time without embellishment. "Did you find out anything useful?"

"I'm afraid not, chief. Nan says she's never seen Brockton."

"What, never?" Pickett asked, his embarrassment forgotten. "But if the fellow wrote his letter from here two days before it arrived in Bow Street, and then it took us another two days to get here—why, he must have been here for five days at the least reckoning!"

Carson shrugged. "Maybe he likes to keep to himself."

"Maybe," Pickett said doubtfully. "But in that case, where is he? He hasn't been in his room."

"Maybe he never wrote from Dunbury at all, but from some other location entirely," Carson continued.

"You may have something there," Pickett conceded. "I'd wondered the same thing myself."

Carson nodded sagely. "Of course you did."

"And just what is that supposed to mean?" demanded Pickett.

Harry's blue eyes grew round with something that was apparently supposed to be innocence. "Why, nothing."

"If you'll recall, I mentioned such a thing to Mr. Colquhoun when he first assigned us to the case," Pickett insisted, unwilling to let the insult pass.

Carson shrugged. "Anything you say, chief."

Pickett was far from satisfied, but recognized he had no choice but to let the matter drop. "Be that as it may, Brockton must have been on the premises by the evening we arrived."

"How do you figure that, sir?" asked Thomas, who had moved to the fire and was now rearranging the two shirts hanging from chairbacks to dry.

"Because the innkeeper's daughter didn't seem at all surprised at our asking for him. If there was no one here registered under that name, surely she would have said so— unless, of course, she took one look at Mr. Carson here and everything else went right out of her head."

Carson grinned appreciatively. "It probably wouldn't be the first time. Nor, hopefully, the last. That's why I don't intend to be taken in by any female for a long, long time."

"My dear Carson," Pickett said pityingly, "what makes you think you'll have any choice in the matter?"

Pickett himself, at least, had not. After a disappointment in his youth (a disappointment which, looking back, he now recognized as a lucky escape) he'd guarded his heart for five long years—until one look at Julia, Lady Fieldhurst, standing pale and frightened over the body of her murdered husband, had crumbled his carefully maintained defenses to dust.

"Someday, some woman is going to make you eat those words," he predicted with a confidence born of experience. "And when she does, I hope I'm there to see it—and laugh."

* * *

Pickett was not laughing the next day, however, when Mr. Edward Gaines Brockton had still not materialized. The more he thought on the matter—and he'd had plenty of opportunity for thinking, as it seemed to be the only thing he could do unless and until he ran his quarry to ground—the more Pickett became convinced that the man's presence in Dunbury had more to do with business than pleasure. "If he had friends or family in the area, surely he must have been staying with them, rather than putting up at an inn." As was his usual habit when deep in thought, he paced the floor, expounding this theory to Harry while Thomas listened in. "It stands to reason, then, that he must have some business here—some legal matter, perhaps, or a commercial enterprise. If you'll recall, I said I thought he might be a merchant, based on his letter."

"And once he arrived, he discovered something havey-cavey about the matter," Harry deduced. Even though Pickett had abandoned the room's only chair, Harry didn't quite dare to stake a claim to it, choosing to remain seated on the edge of the bed.

Pickett nodded. "Very likely."

"So, what's the plan, chief?"

"I want to make a few inquiries before calling on Mrs. Avery this afternoon. You can stay here and try Mr. Brockton's door from time to time. He has to come back to his room sooner or later. In the meantime, you can see what our host can tell you—if you can look the man in the face, after trying to seduce his daughter."

"It's not as if I forced the girl!" protested Harry, all wounded innocence.

Pickett gave him a speaking look, but addressed himself to Thomas. "Keep your ears attuned for any mention of him in the stables—not necessarily Brockton by name, but any complaints about a man coming and going at odd hours, calling for his rig or leaving his horse to be tended at inconvenient times. You need not make any inquiries, but you might put it about that you're in the service of a Bow Street man, and see if they're impressed enough with your credentials to tell you anything. If they do, you're not to make any judgment calls as to whether or not it's important. Tell me anything that's said, or if I'm not here, you may tell Mr. Carson."

"Yes, sir!" Thomas said, all eagerness to be included.

"I'm done with being discreet," Pickett concluded. "We've tried that, and it's got us nowhere. We're going to let it be known who we are and why we're here. If discretion is as important as Mr. Brockton's letter claims, he'll have to come out of hiding long enough to silence us."

Harry squirmed uncomfortably, and the mattress crackled beneath him. "Define 'silence,' chief."

"Unfortunate choice of words," Pickett offered apologetically. "I only meant that he wouldn't want us bandying it about that we've come from Bow Street. I didn't mean to suggest that he might have summoned us here only to kill us."

"I'm relieved to hear it! But what if he *can't* 'come out of hiding'?"

Pickett remembered Carson's suggestion that Brockton might be dead, and realized he didn't want to say the words in front of Thomas. He was surprised—and, yes, relieved—to realize his colleague possessed more circumspection than he'd credited him with.

"In that case, we'll hope the presence of two Bow Street

men in the vicinity makes his enemies very nervous." In a much lighter tone, he turned to his valet. "I'll have the green coat, Thomas, if it isn't too wrinkled from the journey."

"If it is, I'll press it for you, sir," declared Thomas, all eagerness to serve.

"That won't be necessary—" he began, only to be cut short by Carson.

"Of course it is! We can't have you going off to see Mrs. Avery in a wrinkled coat, now, can we?"

Pickett took back every charitable thought he'd had about him.

7

In Which the Hunter Becomes the Hunted

T hankfully, the village of Dunbury was not so large as to offer a great many commercial enterprises, and it boasted even fewer legal offices. Pickett began his search at the local bank, reasoning that this establishment might have a foot in both camps, so to speak. Unfortunately, the clerk he questioned had no knowledge of any person answering to such a name, and when Pickett persuaded him to summon the bank's governor, this individual was able to state with certainty that the institution numbered no one by the name of Brockton among its clients.

The one solicitor charged with handling all the legal business of Dunbury professed the same ignorance, and so Pickett was forced to turn his attention to an odd mix of retail endeavors, from the greengrocer at one end of the High Street to the emporium at the other. Hope surged briefly when he discovered Dunbury numbered a livery stable amongst its commercial endeavors, but this promising lead shriveled and died when the owner of the establishment categorically denied having hired out any of his livestock to anyone by the name of Brockton, then segued into a lengthy diatribe on the dearth of business in a village the size of Dunbury, concluding with his stated intention of trying his luck in nearby Wells. Pickett listened to this speech with every appearance of sympathy, while inwardly conceding that if business were indeed as slow as the man claimed, he would certainly have remembered any visitor from out of town who had hired a hack for a stay of almost a week, and quite possibly more.

Eventually, he had covered every shop in the High Street, and had nothing at all to show for it. It appeared that he would be obliged to pin all his hopes to his meeting with Mrs. Avery. He recalled that her house was in the High Street—on the other end, which necessitated traversing that thoroughfare yet again—and she might well have stood in the window and watched him pass by. The day was warm and the unpaved street was dusty, and Pickett wished he might return to the inn long enough to change his coat and put on a fresh cravat. But aside from the fact that Harry Carson would almost certainly have something to say about that, there was also the possibility that Mrs. Avery had seen him from her window. He would not want her to think he had dressed specially for her, lest she get entirely the wrong impression. And so, stifling the sense that he was somehow betraying Julia by calling on another woman while dressed in the finery she had bestowed upon him as a gift, he trudged back up the High Street and rapped on the door of the last house but one, just past the bookseller's shop.

It was opened to him at once, and not by any servant, but by the lady herself. In fact, no servants were in evidence at all; it was as if they were alone in the house. If the widow truly wanted to avoid becoming the subject of malicious gossip, she certainly had strange ways of going about it.

"Do come in, Mr. Pickett," she said warmly, inviting him to enter with a wave of her hand. "I'm so pleased you finally summoned the courage to knock. I confess, I was beginning to wonder."

The coy smile on her red lips as she closed the door behind him gave Pickett to understand that she had indeed been watching from the window, and that she was laboring under just the misapprehension he had most wished to avoid.

"No, no, it isn't that," he assured her hastily. "I'm in the midst of an investigation, you know. Rather, I *ought* to be in the midst of one; in fact, I've scarcely even begun, for although Mr. Edward Gaines Brockton summoned me here, I've yet to find him. I believe you said you were acquainted with him?"

"You don't waste any time in coming to the point, do you? I wonder, is that a good thing, or a bad one? I daresay time will tell. But come! Let us have our tea, before the water grows cold!"

She led him into a small but elegantly furnished parlor, and after they were seated side by side (and with less space between them than Pickett might have wished) on the gold brocade sofa, she dispensed tea and cakes, all the while pressing him with questions about life in London and asking if he were acquainted with a number of persons whose names he had never heard before.

"I'm afraid we move in different social circles," he confessed. Then, seeing an opening, he added, "And what of Mr. Brockton? In what circles might one expect to meet him—yours, or mine?"

She shrugged her black-clad shoulders. "I really can't say."

" 'Can't,' Mrs. Avery, or 'won't'?" Pickett asked with some asperity, frustrated at being treated more like a favored suitor than a Bow Street investigator.

"Won't," she confessed with a wholly unrepentant smile which might have been charming to a man less impatient to conclude his business and return home to his wife. "I have a feeling that, once you have pumped me for any information I might give you about Mr. Brockton—a man in whom, I confess, I take not the slightest interest—you will have nothing more to say to me. It is very lowering to a woman's *amour propre*, you know." She took the teacup from his unresisting hand and set it on the small table at her elbow, then slid her hands up his arms to his shoulders, whereupon she groped for the end of his cravat and tugged the knot loose.

"Look here," Pickett said, no longer bothering to hide his growing impatience as he edged away from her toward his own end of the sofa, "you told me yesterday that if I would call on you, you would tell me about Mr. Brockton. Well, here I am. So—talk."

"I'm afraid your memory is faulty, Mr. Pickett. What I said was that if you would come to tea, I would make it worth your while." And, having delivered herself of this speech, she seized Pickett by the ears, pulled his head down, and plastered her lips to his.

"I am a married man, Mrs. Avery!" he protested, prying her loose with an effort, "If this was what you intended, you would have done better to issue your invitation to my colleague, Harry Carson!"

Deprived of her primary object, Mrs. Avery gave a little huff of annoyance. "I thank you, but no! Men like your Mr. Carson may be found under every bush—usually in the company of some village lass or farmer's daughter. I have no desire to become a notch on his bedpost."

"No, you would prefer that I become a notch on yours."

She gave him a rather pitying smile. "You do yourself less than justice, Mr. Pickett."

"Be that as it may, I came to Dunbury for one purpose, and one purpose only: to find Edward Gaines Brockton—"

"Do you know, I am becoming very tired of hearing that name?"

"—and to discover why he summoned me from Bow Street. If you have no information to offer on the subject—"

"I believe that makes two," she said.

"I—I beg your pardon?"

"You said you came for one purpose alone, but you named two." She ticked them off on her fingers. "To find this man Brockton—that is one—and to discover why he had sent for you—that makes two. Dare I hope to interest you in a third?"

Seeing that she had every intention of advancing upon him again, Pickett leaped to his feet. It took some doing, since she was determined to keep him there, but at last he was able to make good his escape, none the worse for his experiences beneath the amorous Widow Avery's roof.

Or so he thought. He was soon disabused of this notion. He returned to the Cock and Boar to find Carson and Thomas there. Both young men looked up at his entrance, and Harry grinned with fiendish delight.

"Productive afternoon at Mrs. Avery's?" he asked, giving Pickett a knowing look.

"*Ahem!*"

Thomas cleared his throat, and Pickett's gaze shifted from Carson to the valet standing some little distance behind him. Having gained his master's attention, he tapped his finger against the corner of his mouth. Pickett glanced toward the mirror mounted over the washstand, and the reason for Carson's unholy glee became clear. The corner of Pickett's mouth was smudged with Mrs. Avery's lip-rouge and his cravat was untied, the loose ends hanging down over the front of his waistcoat. In fact, he looked thoroughly debauched. Worse, he had walked all the way down the High Street in this condition. Worst of all, Dunbury was near enough to Norwood Green that Julia's parents might have acquaintances in the town.

There was no help for it: he would have to write to her that very day and make a clean breast of the matter, before word reached her from some other source—including the one standing before him. In the meantime, there was nothing for it but to put on a brave face.

"Productive? I'm afraid not," he said with as nonchalant

an air as he could manage, under the circumstances. He crossed the small room to the washstand, poured water—now cold—from the pitcher into the bowl and began to scrub the evidence of the widow's amorous assault from his mouth. "I'm afraid Mrs. Avery was less interested in the investigation than she was in the investigator. And Thomas, I'll be the one to tell Mrs. Pickett about this, if you please."

"Of course, sir," Thomas, who had been Julia's footman when she was still Lady Fieldhurst, readily agreed.

"As for Mr. Brockton," Pickett continued, "I'm beginning to wonder if Mrs. Avery knows anything about him at all."

Carson made some remark about some fellows having all the luck, but Pickett, only half listening, made no reply. In fact, the suspicion that Mrs. Avery knew nothing of their quarry was not the most far-fetched of the theories beginning to form in his brain. And that very night, he intended to put one of them to the test.

* * *

While Pickett fended off the lascivious lady, Julia was undergoing a trial of quite another kind. For it was the day of her tea-party, the event that was to mark her re-entry, in a small way, to the society in which she had moved before the murder of her first husband and the marriage to her second. It was ridiculous, in a way, that she should be in such a perturbation of spirits over entertaining some half-dozen ladies to tea—she, who had once been a political hostess of some note, having arranged dinners whose guest lists had included various Foreign Office dignitaries, Members of

Parliament, and even, on one momentous occasion, the Prince of Wales himself. After such rarified company, half a dozen ladies of the *ton* should have no power to terrify.

She had already suffered a small setback in the form of a letter from the elderly Lady Oversley, expressing her regrets due to a toothache of sufficient severity to render her unable to rise from her bed, and closing her correspondence with the hope that she might avail herself of Mrs. Pickett's hospitality at some future date. Julia accepted this reversal of fortune with some misgivings. She did her ladyship the justice to own that her toothache was very likely quite genuine, for when she had seen Lady Oversley in church the previous morning, the dowager marchioness had professed herself to be looking forward to the event.

Still, Julia felt somewhat as if the floor had begun to give beneath her feet. Her dearest friend Emily, Lady Dunnington was not in residence in Town at present, having recently been brought to bed of a daughter—her first girl after presenting her husband with two boys—and feeling quite satisfied with herself, if her letters were anything to judge by. In Lady Dunnington's absence, Julia had counted upon the presence of Lady Oversley, who had herself benefited from the expertise of Bow Street's principal officers only a few months earlier, and who might (she hoped) have been depended on to support Julia in case her other guests should choose to express their disapproval of, if not outright scorn for, their hostess's second marriage.

Now, as the echoes of the longcase clock sounding the hour began to fade, she rose from her place on the sofa and began to pace restlessly about the drawing room, pausing from time to time in order to make minuscule (and wholly unnecessary) adjustments to the arrangement of cakes on a silver tray, or to pluck a stray leaf or petal from the bouquets of flowers purchased fresh that morning from the floral markets of Covent Garden.

The ticking of the clock seemed unnaturally loud in the still house, to such an extent that when it chimed the quarter-hour, the sound was sufficient to make Julia start. *It is too soon to worry*, she reasoned. The traffic in Mayfair on a Monday could be heavy enough to make anyone late, as the delivery wagons of merchants obliged to remain idle the previous day in honor of the Sabbath now scrambled to make up for lost time. Perhaps the mistake had been hers, for scheduling her party on a Monday instead of waiting until later in the week. But she had not wanted to wait, hoping against hope that her husband would have returned before the end of the week. If that should prove to be the case, she would not want him to be made uncomfortable were he to walk into the drawing room with his valise and find himself in the middle of a ladies' tea party. *Nor*, a little voice whispered, *would you want him to suffer any mortification, should the party be a failure and he the unwitting cause.*

When the clock chimed half past two, she recalled a book lying on the bedside table upstairs, and wondered if she might send Andrew, the footman, to fetch it. But no, she reasoned, it would not do to have one's guests ushered into the room just in time to see one stuffing Mrs. Radcliffe behind the sofa cushions.

By the time the clock struck a quarter to three, she was so thoroughly bored with her own company that she yielded to impulse and dispatched Andrew on the errand; surely, she decided, anyone with no more courtesy than to make an appearance a full forty-five minutes late deserved no better.

When the Whittington chimes announced the three o'clock hour, her pacing was interrupted by Rogers, who called her attention to his presence with a soft clearing of his throat.

"Begging your pardon, ma'am" he said, and although his tone was scrupulously correct, Julia thought she read something of silent sympathy in his eyes. "I was wondering if there was anything else you needed. Shall I refresh the hot water for the tea, perhaps?" His gaze shifted from her to the teapot; the water it held would by this time certainly be tepid.

"Actually, there is," she said, much too brightly. "It appears that you and the rest of the servants have quite a treat in store. Pray take these things downstairs and share them with the staff, with my compliments."

He opened his mouth as if to say something, then shut it, moved toward the tea table, and finally spoke again. "All of it, ma'am? Are you certain you would not like to make up a plate and pour a cup of tea for yourself first?"

"To tell you the truth, I am heartily sick of looking at it," she confessed. "Only, pray, do not tell Cook I said so, for she worked so hard on it all!"

"Yes, ma'am." He picked up the tray and took two steps toward the door before pausing and turning back. "If you will pardon my presumption in saying so, ma'am, you made the better bargain."

She did not have to ask for an explanation. Rogers, at least, had never wondered at her choosing to marry a man so far beneath her socially, for he, too, stood in his debt. A sudden longing for her husband's return lanced through her like a knife to the heart. "Yes," she said, blinking back the tears that filled her eyes. "Yes, I did."

Whatever the butler might have said to this was interrupted by a knock on the door.

"If you will excuse me, ma'am."

He set the tray back down and left the room. Julia strained her ears to identify which of her guests had put in an arrival, however tardy, but the faint voices that reached her seemed to be masculine. Suddenly there came the sound of scuffling feet.

"Andrew—!" Rogers shouted for the footman, but his voice broke off abruptly, followed in rapid succession by a dull thud and a crash.

"Rogers?" Julia called, hurrying into the foyer. "Rogers, are you—?"

She stopped, staring. Rogers lay in a heap on the floor, bright red blood running down his graying hair to pool on the white marble tiles. A man stood over him, a man of about thirty clad in rough clothes and holding a stout wooden cudgel.

"Who are you, and why are you here?" Julia demanded with more bravado than she felt.

"Never mind," he said in an accent she couldn't place. "You just come with me, and no one will get hurt."

"It's a little late for that, don't you think?" she retorted, gesturing toward the butler's still form. "Leave this house at once!"

"Not without you, I won't."

With his free hand, he seized her by the arm. She tried to twist out of his hold, but he was too strong. When the sound of running footsteps on the stairs heralded the imminent arrival of Andrew, her attacker wrapped his other arm—the one holding the cudgel—around her and began dragging her toward the door. Julia fought with every weapon at her disposal, kicking at his legs and even sinking her teeth into his arm, but to no avail.

"I hate to cosh a female," he grumbled to no one in particular.

Then the cudgel came down on her head, and Julia knew no more. The man hefted her over his shoulder as if she were a sack of grain and carried her out to the waiting carriage.

Andrew arrived just in time to see the vehicle bowling away down Curzon Street.

8

*In Which the Investigation
Takes a Most Unexpected Turn*

C arson!" Pickett hissed, shaking the slumbering form
beside him with enough force to cause the pea-
shuckings beneath him to crackle. "Carson, wake up!"

"Huh—what—?" Gradually Harry's sleep-fogged brain
registered the owner of the hand closed about his shoulder.
"Confound it, Mr. Pickett, do you have any idea what time it
is?"

"Just past three, if the clock over the stable is correct,"
replied Pickett, unrepentant.

"Oh, is that all? And I suppose you think it's a good time
for a stroll before breakfast," Harry grumbled, preparing to
roll back over and resume his interrupted slumber.

"No, but I think it's a very good time to make the
acquaintance of Mr. Edward Gaines Brockton."

"If he has any sense, he'll tell you to go to the devil!"

"On the contrary, I don't think he'll tell me anything,"

Pickett predicted.

"Then why bother knocking him up at all?"

"You said yourself that you wondered if he might be dead," Pickett reminded him. "Wouldn't you like to find out?"

Yielding to the inevitable, Harry sat up with a sigh, casting one longing glance back at his pillow before reaching for his breeches. His superior, he noticed, was already dressed, albeit sketchily, with a dark coat and breeches pulled on over his shirt. He wore no cravat, and his feet were bare.

"I want to make as little noise as possible," Pickett explained, apparently conscious of this unflattering appraisal. "Put on your stockings, if you like, but no shoes."

"If you can go capering about in your bare feet, I suppose I can," Harry said without enthusiasm, standing up to stuff the tail of his shirt into his breeches. "Although if you should find yourself confronting an angry man in his nightshirt, it'll be no more than you deserve."

"If that should prove to be the case, I'll hide behind you." As Pickett stood fully half a head taller than his colleague, this promise drew a reluctant grin from Harry. "Besides, *he's* the one who sent for *us*, remember? If he won't open his door during the day, he can hardly blame us for trying our luck at night."

"All right, chief, you've convinced me. But it seems to me that you could do the thing just as well by yourself. Now that you've dragged me out of bed at this ungodly hour, what do you want me to do?"

"No, not that yellow monstrosity you wore on the stage," Pickett objected as Harry began to shrug on his mustard-colored coat. "Wear something darker."

" 'Monstrosity'? I'll have you know this coat is the height of fashion—well, as much fashion as you can get for three and six," Harry amended, reluctantly reaching for the blue coat that constituted part of his uniform. "We don't all have a viscountess ready to turn us out like a tulip of fashion, you know."

Pickett knew. In fact, the wardrobe Julia had seen fit to bestow upon him had been a considerable bone of contention between them, but he had no intention of making Harry Carson a gift of this information.

"Stubble it, will you? I'm about to open the door," he said, and suited the word to the deed.

Nothing moved in the corridor, and no light showed beneath any of the doors. He motioned silently for Harry to follow, and stepped out into the corridor. They traversed the short distance to the next room, but when Harry raised his closed fist to knock on the door, Pickett put out a hand to forestall him.

"I don't want to give him any warning," he whispered.

"Yes, but we have him trapped," Harry pointed out. "There's no other exit."

"There's a window, with a tree growing right outside it," Pickett reminded him. "Now, keep an eye out for anyone coming up the stairs."

In spite of these instructions, Harry stared in bewilderment as Pickett dropped to one knee and inserted a long, narrow instrument—a lady's hairpin, by the looks of it—into the lock and put his ear to it.

"What are you—?"

"Shh!" Pickett silenced him. "I'm trying to listen—there it is!"

And so saying, he eased the door open.

"Now, there's a neat trick," Harry said in grudging admiration. He jerked his thumb in the general direction of London and, presumably, magistrate Patrick Colquhoun. "Does the boss know you can do that?"

"He knows," Pickett replied cryptically.

"Can you teach me how?"

"Shh!" Pickett said again.

He stepped into the dark little room and moved aside for Harry to follow, then closed the door behind them. The moon was a couple of days past the full, but enough moonlight filtered through the thin curtain to reveal that the bed was empty.

"Our friend Mr. Brockton keeps late hours," Harry grumbled. "Still, I suppose it's better than discovering him lying in the bed stabbed to death. So, chief, what happens now? Do we wait for him?"

"I think we'd be waiting a long time," Pickett said, groping on the bedside table for the flint. He found it, and a moment later the candle in its brass holder flared to life.

"Meaning?" prompted Harry.

"I don't think he's ever been here at all."

"But—but the innkeeper said—"

"I don't doubt that there's someone listed on the inn's registry as Edward Gaines Brockton," said Pickett, readily conceding the point. "But does it not strike you as a bit odd that no one recalls actually seeing the man, or speaking to him?"

"Nan told us this morning that he'd gone to church," Harry reminded him. "She must have got that information from somewhere."

Pickett shook his head. "She speculated that he must have done so, based on the fact that he wasn't in his room on a Sunday morning. But when you pressed her for details, she admitted that she's never actually seen him."

He turned back to the candle and picked it up. Weird shadows danced on the walls as he held it aloft, bathing the corners of the room in a yellow glow. No valise stood against the wall, and no personal effects had been arranged on the wash stand.

"Let's see what we have here," he said, crossing to the clothes-press in three strides.

"You don't intend to go through the fellow's undergarments!" Harry protested.

"I wish I could, but I have a feeling I can't," Pickett replied, and opened its doors.

Several round wooden pegs had been affixed to the inside walls of the clothespress, but no garments hung from them. Nor did Pickett hold out much hope for the three drawers in the bottom of the piece, but he had to try.

"Here, hold this," he said, handing the candle to his colleague.

"Well, if that don't beat the Dutch!" exclaimed Harry, taking the candle nevertheless. "There's such a thing as privacy, you know!"

"Let me remind you that *he* sent for *us*," Pickett said, not for the first time. "If one summons a Runner—much less two!—from Bow Street, one should expect that some information is going to be required. If he won't, or can't, give me the information himself, no one can blame me for getting it by whatever method I have at my disposal. At least, they can't blame me much," he amended, trying not to think of what Mr. Colquhoun might think of this particular method.

While Harry pondered this claim, Pickett eased the top drawer open. The piece was old, and the groan of ill-fitting wood sliding against wood sounded unnaturally loud in the darkness.

"Empty," he pronounced with a sigh of resignation, if not surprise.

The other two drawers proved to be no more helpful.

"I've heard of traveling light, but surely no one travels *that* light," Harry complained. "If he did—if he'd been wearing the same clothes for, what, three days, to say nothing of not shaving—surely the good people of Dunbury would smell him coming at twenty paces."

"Think, Carson," Pickett chided. "You're not stupid, although it amuses you sometimes to pretend to be. I doubt anyone has been in this room at all for the past week." He ran a finger along the top edge of the clothespress, and examined the fine coating of dust that covered it. "It's for certain no one has cleaned it."

"That doesn't necessarily mean anything," Carson pointed out. "Not every hostelry is as fastidious as you seem to expect."

"No, but if anyone had been staying in this room, don't you think he would have touched something? If not the clothespress, then surely the bedside table."

Carson glanced toward the article of furniture in question. "You can see it from here? I know the room is small, but surely—"

"No one's vision is that good," Pickett said, amused in spite of the circumstances. He almost hated to admit it; he needed all the ammunition against Harry Carson that he could get. "I noticed it when I picked up the candle It left a clean circle where no dust could reach."

"All right, then, I guess you've convinced me," Carson conceded the point, although it clearly went against the grain with him to do so. "Where does that leave us?"

"I'll have a word with the innkeeper in the morning. Until then, we should get what sleep we can. Tomorrow may be a long day."

He could not have known how prophetic the words would prove.

* * *

Having returned to his bed, Pickett lay on his back, staring up at the ceiling and listening to the faint sounds of Carson snoring. He was missing something; he was sure of it. He just couldn't think what it might be. Finally, abandoning all attempts at slumber, he threw back the bedclothes and padded across the room to where his coat hung over the back of the chair drawn up beneath the writing table. He groped until he located a folded sheet of paper in the inside coat pocket, then sat down in the chair and lit the candle, positioning it so that his body blocked the light from reaching Carson. Not, he reflected bitterly, that anything less than an exploding grenade was capable of rousing Carson once sleep had claimed him.

Here, however, it appeared Pickett had misjudged him.

"What're you doin' now," Carson asked sleepily.

"Nothing," Pickett said. "Just testing a theory."

"D'you always test your theories in the middle of the night?"

"Only when they keep me awake. Go back to sleep, Carson."

Moments later, the heavy breathing emitting from beneath the bedclothes gave Pickett to understand that his subordinate had taken these instructions to heart. Pickett, meanwhile, had spread the paper open, and now studied the message written upon it.

To Patrick Colquhoun, Esq., it read, *I am writing to request that you send two of your best men to attend me at the Cock and Boar in Dunbury regarding a matter of some delicacy. I further request that one of these men be Mr. John Pickett, who distinguished himself last winter in the matter of the jewel thefts occurring at the Drury Lane Theatre. The second man I shall leave to your own choosing. If Mr. Pickett is on assignment elsewhere at present, please send word to me at the aforementioned hostelry so that I may arrange to meet with him at some future date.* It was signed, *Yr Most Obedient Servant, Edward Gaines Brockton.*

Perhaps he should have been flattered, Pickett thought, that the writer had asked for him so specifically, even to the extent of delaying his request until Pickett should be available. And yet, he didn't feel flattered, and he didn't believe his uneasiness could be attributed only to modesty.

Obeying the whim that had roused him from his bed, he held the paper over the candle flame until his hands grew uncomfortably warm, then peered closely at the letter. No faint brown markings emerged to indicate a hidden message communicated in a secret code. The letter was exactly what it appeared to be: a request for two men to investigate a case of sufficient sensitivity that the writer refused to commit it to paper. It might be anything from the theft of the family jewels to the elopement of the man's daughter to Gretna Green with a fortune-hunter.

But no, Pickett reasoned, surely if that were the case, the man would take whoever might be available to travel at a moment's notice, and be thankful for him. What sort of case would be of sufficient importance to require two men, but of so little urgency that it might wait upon his own convenience?

Pickett had no answers. He refolded the letter, but as he did so, his gaze fell upon the man's signature. *Edward Gaines Brockton.* Surely it was only a coincidence that the initials were the same as those in the letter that had summoned him to the Lake District: *E. G. B.* In that earlier case, the initials had not represented a name at all, but *Éire go Brách*—the rallying cry of those who supported the cause of Irish independence. But there was nothing in the letter to suggest that Brockton had any interest in the Irish, and the man who had written that earlier letter was now imprisoned in Carlisle, awaiting execution for treason. The similarity was no more than an unsettling coincidence.

It had to be.

The alternative was too terrible to contemplate.

* * *

The following morning, Pickett awoke from a troubled sleep and tarried only long enough to dress, shave, and eat a rudimentary breakfast before approaching the innkeeper.

"No trouble with your lodgings, I hope," said this worthy, no doubt seeing the thoughtful crease puckering his guest's brow and assuming the worst.

"No, not at all," Pickett assured him. "But we came from London to meet with a Mr. Edward Gaines Brockton, and neither we nor anyone else appears to have seen him."

Their host shook his head. "I'm afraid you must add me to the list. I haven't seen him, either."

"Was your daughter minding the desk when he arrived, then?" asked Pickett, baffled. "I believe she gave my colleague the opposite impression, when he questioned her on the matter. A misunderstanding, perhaps?" Of course, at the time of the questioning she had been either defending her virtue or assisting Carson in relieving her of it, but he had no intention of pointing this out to the girl's father.

"There was no misunderstanding," the innkeeper said. "I was minding the desk at the time, but I never saw the fellow, for he didn't come in and hire the room himself."

"Oh? Then how—?"

"A lady came in and asked that a room be kept ready for her friend who would be arriving, what, four days ago now— this Friday last. Give me half a crown in advance, she did, for holding the room until he arrived. So I wrote his name down in the book and told my Nan not to be giving that room to no one else."

"I see," Pickett said thoughtfully, although this explanation didn't answer all his questions, not by a long chalk. It might account for how the elusive Mr. Brockton had managed to procure a room without ever showing his face, but it offered no clue as to why the room was empty, four days after Brockton had supposedly taken possession of it. "And did he arrive last Friday, as expected?"

The innkeeper scratched his chin. "I suppose he must have. Neither me nor Nan saw him come in, mind, but the lady stopped by that morning to fetch the key to his room." He glanced over his shoulder at the wall behind him, upon which had been mounted a wooden structure divided into some half-dozen pigeonholes. Some of these were empty, while others held what appeared, at this distance and from this angle, a single brass key in each compartment. "I expect he was a relation, and intended to stop at her house first. Or maybe he didn't expect to reach Dunbury until late, and didn't want to rouse the house."

"And the lady who requested the room?" Pickett prompted. "Do you know her name?"

"Aye, that I do. It were Mrs. Avery."

"*Mrs. Avery?*" Pickett echoed, dumbfounded. "The widow, Mrs. Avery?"

"Aye. You know her?"

"We've met," Pickett said tersely. "Thank you for the information. I'm obliged to you."

He didn't bother to go back upstairs to inform Carson of his discovery, but set out at a brisk walk for Mrs. Avery's house at the opposite end of the High Street.

"Why, Mr. Pickett, what a pleasant surprise," she purred when the housemaid—who had been conspicuous by her absence the day before—showed him into the parlor.

"Is it?" Pickett asked, with none of the blushing confusion that he had shown on his previous visit. "I'm afraid you may not find it so for long."

"False modesty, Mr. Pickett," she chided, and although her manner was flirtatious, her expression grew wary.

"Mrs. Avery, less than twenty-four hours ago and in this very room, you deflected every question I asked you about Edward Gaines Brockton—"

"But I don't know anything!" she protested, opening her blue eyes wide. "I've never met the man!"

" 'Never'? Then how is it that you reserved a room for him at the Cock and Boar?"

She gestured toward the sofa. "Pray sit down, Mr. Pickett, and allow me to explain."

"Forgive me if I choose to remain standing," Pickett replied, hardening his heart. "I know only too well what happens to men who sit next to you."

She sighed. "You misjudge me, Mr. Pickett, but I suppose it is no more than I deserve. In fact, I can tell you very little about Mr. Brockton. I have never met him, you see."

"You've never met the man, and yet you reserve a room for him at the Cock and Boar," Pickett said skeptically. "Why don't you pull the other one, Mrs. Avery? It's got bells on."

"It's true!" she insisted. "If you must know, I—I answered an advertisement in the newspaper."

"You answered an advertisement in the newspaper," Pickett echoed, not quite certain if she were still having him on or not.

"I am a widow, Mr. Pickett," she reminded him. "My late husband did not leave me lavishly provided for, and genteel options for supplementing a lady's income are few. When I saw an advertisement requesting assistance in making arrangements for a traveler, it seemed a simple enough request."

"Who placed the advertisement? Was it Mr. Brockton?"

"I don't know," she confessed with a lift of her black-clad shoulders. "He never gave his name."

"He never sent you a bank draft for holding up your end of the bargain?"

"He sent me a ten-pound note. It was torn in half, and the two pieces sent separately through the post."

Pickett nodded. Mail theft was a common problem, and the solution Mrs. Avery described—that of tearing or cutting banknotes in half and thus rendering them worthless unless one were in possession of both halves—was not unusual in itself. Still . . .

"Ten pounds is a lot to pay in return for one small favor—"

"Two small favors, actually. I was also charged with collecting the key to the room on Friday, the day he was to have arrived."

"Two, then," Pickett amended impatiently, "and he

seems to have gone to great lengths not to reveal anything about himself, or his whereabouts. And yet it never occurred to you that there might be anything havey-cavey about the business?"

"Beggars cannot afford to be choosers, Mr. Pickett," she pointed out. "There was nothing illegal in what I was asked to do, and he was offering to pay me very well in return for only a very minor inconvenience." She sighed. "Mr. Pickett, may we not sit down? It is a long story, and I should prefer to make myself comfortable before I tell it. I promise, I shall make no untoward advances upon your person," she added with more than a hint of asperity.

Pickett consented, and once they were seated on the sofa, she picked up the thread of her story. "You asked if I never questioned the ethics, if not the legality, of what I was requested to do. In fact, it was not until I saw you in church and realized Bow Street was taking an interest in the matter that I began to wonder. That, and the fact that Mr. Brockton had apparently never reached Dunbury, made me think I might have got more than I bargained for."

"You recognized my colleague's uniform," Pickett observed.

She nodded. "Mr. Avery and I lived in London for a short time following our marriage, and I am familiar with the costume of the Bow Street Horse Patrol—though not from any personal run-ins with the law, you understand. When I overheard you asking the vicar about Mr. Brockton—well, you may imagine the thoughts that ran through my head. I am not wholly without principles, you know. I had to discover if

I had unwittingly become some sort of accessory to a crime. To that end, I inserted myself into your conversation with the vicar, and asked him for an introduction."

"And yet when you invited me to tea, you implied that you possessed some information that would be of interest to me," he reminded her.

"Obviously I did possess such information, or you would not be here now," she pointed out. "Still, the purpose of my invitation was not to impart information, but to obtain it."

"Oh, was that it? You'll forgive me for thinking the purpose of your invitation was something entirely different."

"Yes, but you would not follow the rules of the game, Mr. Pickett," she chided. "Had you followed the rules, we would have spent a very pleasant afternoon upstairs, at the end of which you—by this time thoroughly sated with food, wine, and me—would have confided the nature of your business in Dunbury. If you had said, 'I am to have the honor of informing Mr. Brockton that he is heir to a fortune in the West Indies,' I would have obligingly told you all that I knew. On the other hand, if you had said, 'I must arrest Mr. Brockton for murder and bring him back to London in irons,' I would have held my tongue."

This last was confessed with so charming a smile that it required some effort on Pickett's part not to return it. "If that was what you had in mind, you would have done better to address your attentions to my colleague, Mr. Carson—as I believe I told you at the time."

She gave a disdainful sniff. "Yes, and I told you what I thought of your Mr. Carson. Besides, if he had told me anything at all, it would no doubt have been so inflated and embroidered—so as to represent him in the best possible light, you understand—that I would have found them utterly worthless."

Her reading of Harry Carson's character was so accurate that Pickett's smile broke free in spite of his best efforts to appear stern and unyielding. "Mrs. Avery, you are an astute judge of human nature."

The widow put her hand to her eyes as if shielding them from the sun. "Pray do not smile at me, Mr. Pickett. It only taunts me with visions of what I cannot have. Yes, that's it! Your blushes are much better."

Ignoring these assurances (which, in fact, had caused him to blush still more deeply crimson), Pickett asked, "Do you still have the newspaper? The one with the advertisement, I mean."

"Why, no. I saw no reason to keep it," she added apologetically.

"What paper was it? The *Times*?"

"No. I daresay he would not bother to advertise in London, since it would require someone here in Dunbury, or within easy reach of it, to carry out the errand. It was the *Wells Journal*."

"I see," Pickett said, contemplating with a sinking heart the necessity of journeying to Wells in search of the publisher of this periodical. "I appreciate your frankness, Mrs. Avery. If you wish, I can return Mr. Brockton's room key to the Cock and Boar for you."

"I would be obliged to you, Mr. Pickett." She rose and

crossed the room to an elegant escritoire, then retrieved a brass key from its shallow top drawer and surrendered it into his keeping. "I only hope you will not be obliged to pay for the room."

"If I am, I will pass the expense along to the Bow Street Public Office. From there, it will be charged to Mr. Brockton. He already owes a substantial sum for two Runners and their traveling expenses."

Of course, there was the little matter of finding him first, but Pickett had every confidence in his magistrate; when it came to collecting remuneration, Mr. Colquhoun lived up to his Scottish heritage.

"May I ask a favor of you, Mr. Pickett?" the widow asked, accompanying him to the door. "Will you let me know what you discover about the man? I confess to being curious, and perhaps even a little worried about him."

"It's very likely nothing more than someone's idea of a joke," Pickett assured her, and tried hard to believe it. And yet, there was the troubling coincidence of those initials . . . Still, he couldn't help feeling a bit sorry for Mrs. Avery, whose life was so circumscribed that she was reduced to answering anonymous advertisements for money and seducing random visitors for amusement. "If I should prove to be wrong, I will let you know."

With this promise, he took his leave and began retracing his route up the High Street toward the Cock and Boar. He passed the bookseller's shop and was approaching the livery stable when the sound of thundering hoofbeats behind him caused him to press closer to the buildings. He looked up to glare at the passing rider, and suffered a check. The man on horseback wore the blue coat and red waistcoat, both now liberally coated with dust, of the Bow Street Horse Patrol. Even as his brain registered this curious fact, the two men's eyes met as the sweating horse raced past in a cloud of dust. The rider wheeled his mount 'round, and returned to Pickett.

"Mr. Pickett—thank God—I found you—" Samuel Matthews was almost as winded as the horse beneath him. He reached into his dusty coat and retrieved a folded and sealed paper. "This—for you—Mr. Colquhoun—"

Pickett didn't waste time asking questions the man clearly didn't have the breath to answer. He took the paper, and noticed that it was actually two sheets folded together. He broke the seal, then opened it and scanned the scrawled lines.

"Mr. Pickett?" asked Matthews, seeing the face of his Bow Street compatriot turn white as death.

"It's Julia." Pickett spoke like one in a daze. "My wife. She's been abducted."

9

In Which John Pickett Calls In the Cavalry

*Y*ou should have known . . . You should have known . . .
The accusation rang in Pickett's head as he stared at the creased papers in his hands.

"Mr. Pickett?" Matthews's voice seemed to be calling to him from somewhere far away. "Are you all right, sir?"

Pickett looked up, blinking at him as if surprised to see him still there. "My wife," he said in a voice strangely unlike his own. "She's gone."

Matthews slid from the saddle and looped the reins over the horse's head. "Are you going back to the inn—what was it, the Cock and Boar? I'll walk with you."

In fact, he was reluctant to ride ahead and leave Mr. Pickett to make even so short a trek alone. He hadn't been with Bow Street for very long, but he knew that Pickett was regarded there as something of a prodigy, having been promoted from the Foot Patrol to Principal Officer at the age of twenty-three. In the fellow's present state, however,

Matthews wasn't sure he trusted him not to step out in front of a wagon. Once they reached the inn, however—a walk completed in absolute silence, as Pickett had spoken not a word—Matthews was obliged to part company.

"I have to see to Bruno here," he said apologetically, transferring the reins to his other hand so that he might stroke the horse's twitching neck. "I've ridden the poor old fellow hard over the last twenty-four hours, and he deserves some cosseting. I'll be inside shortly, as soon as I've settled him in the stable."

Pickett said nothing, but continued to put one foot in front of the other until he entered the inn. Nancy was behind the counter, so it was hardly surprising that Carson was there as well, leaning against the counter with his chin propped on his hand. Upon seeing Pickett's expression, he stood up straighter, abandoning, at least for the nonce, all interest in his latest flirt.

"You found him, then?" he asked urgently. "Is he dead?"

"She's gone," Pickett said, as if he didn't quite believe the words coming from his own mouth.

"Who? Mrs. Avery?"

"Julia—my wife. She's gone," he said again, as if the words would make sense if only he repeated them often enough.

" 'Gone'? What do you mean, 'gone'?" As the significance of this declaration began to dawn, Carson's blue eyes grew wide. "But that makes you a wealthy widower! Now you can—"

He got no further. Pickett, suddenly awakened from his

stupor, lunged for him. The force of the attack bore both men across the counter and onto the floor on the other side, where they landed in a heap at Nancy's feet. She screamed and, seeing no other way to prevail upon Pickett to detach his hands from about her swain's throat, snatched up a broom and began beating him about the head and shoulders with it.

The commotion was sufficient to reach the upper floor and the ears of Thomas, who had been engaged in putting away his master's newly laundered shirts. Upon hearing evidence of a donnybrook below, he came clattering down the stairs to discover what was in the wind and, if necessary, to lend his aid.

"Thank God!" Nancy looked up from her broom to appeal to the newcomer. "Can't you do something to separate them?"

Finding his master apparently locked in mortal combat with the colleague with whom he had seemingly been on good terms only that morning, Thomas didn't hesitate to join the fray, although not without being accidentally whacked with a broom for his pains.

"Put that thing down, woman!" he commanded Nancy, then set about pulling Pickett off Carson, who was certainly getting the worst of the encounter. Having achieved this goal, however, Thomas didn't hesitate to make it clear on whose side his loyalties lay. "What's he done, sir?" he asked, indicating by his tone that he would be more than willing to pick up where his master had left off, should circumstances dictate such a course of action.

"I didn't do anything!" retorted Carson, picking himself

up and dusting himself off as the color in his face gradually returned to normal. "He just tore into me like a lunatic—and let me tell you, *Mister* Pickett, that if you think your seniority give you the right to—"

"Leave it, Harry."

All four of the participants turned as a fifth person entered the inn, a man in the uniform, albeit sadly dust-covered, of the Bow Street Horse Patrol.

"Matthews?" Carson asked incredulously. "What the devil are *you* doing here?"

Matthews didn't answer at once. His spurs jingled as he crossed the room to address himself to Nancy. "Pour this man a tot of the strongest thing you have," he said with a nod toward Pickett, panting and miserable but making no effort to free himself from Thomas's grasp. "Better make it a double."

"Why isn't anyone ordering drinks for *me?*" Harry grumbled, massaging his abused throat. "Seems to me that *I'm* the injured party here."

"Shut up, Harry," said Pickett and Matthews in unison.

Thomas, seeing his duty clear, ordered a pint of ale for himself and one for each of the Bow Street men, trusting that his master would reimburse him for the expense once the matter, whatever it was, had been settled.

After the drinks had been served, the four men seated themselves around a table near the window. Matthews took a long pull from his tankard, then wiped the foam from his lips with his sleeve, leaving a streak of dust across the lower half of his face.

"First of all, Harry, you'll have to excuse Mr. Pickett. I'd just brought him some bad news." He glanced at the man who, although several years his junior, was nevertheless his superior at Bow Street. "Do you want to tell it, sir, or shall I?" Pickett, staring blindly out the window, sighed deeply, as if he were suddenly tired of living. "My wife has been abducted. She was taken from her house—*our* house—on Monday." Would that have been yesterday, he wondered, or the day before? Time seemed to have suddenly ceased to exist. "Mr. Colquhoun received word on Sunday morning that Robert Hetherington had escaped from prison. Although he's careful to point out that there's no evidence to indicate that the two events are related, he thinks"—he swallowed past the lump in his throat—"he thinks I will probably agree that the timing is a bit too significant for mere coincidence."

"*Do* you?" Carson asked. "Agree, I mean."

"Yes," Pickett said bleakly.

Carson opened his mouth to request some further explanation but, in a rare moment of sensitivity, changed his mind, electing to take a swig of ale instead.

"Begging your pardon, sir," Thomas asked, "but how do they know she was abducted? Couldn't she have just decided to go to her folks' instead?"

Her folks, Pickett recalled, closing his eyes at the thought of this fresh disaster. Her parents, Sir Thaddeus and Lady Runyon, who lived not far from Dunbury, and who he had thought to call on while he was in the area. Now he would have to look them in the eye and tell them that their daughter's life was in danger and that he, who had professed to love her and vowed to care for her, was responsible.

Aloud, however, he merely said, "It's all in the letter. Mr. Colquhoun included Andrew's statement." This, in fact, was the second sheet of paper, which he handed across the table to Thomas. Carson, not to be left out, leaned nearer and read over his shoulder while Pickett summarized for Matthews' benefit. "Andrew is a footman. He was downstairs when he heard Rogers—that's the butler—shout for him, followed by a loud noise like a body"—his voice shook on the word—"hitting the ground. He ran upstairs to find Rogers lying on the floor, bleeding from a head wound. The front door was ajar, and he ran out onto the portico just in time to see the door of an unmarked carriage close, and the driver whip up the horses. He started to run after it, but was soon left behind."

Matthews frowned thoughtfully. "Then how does he know she was inside? What if she just happened to step out of the house at the same time, and this Andrew fellow assumed the worst? Maybe the men in the carriage were even watching for her to leave the house so they could rob it, and—what?" he asked, seeing Pickett shake his head.

"It's there in the written statement. A scrap of fabric was caught in the door of the carriage—light green, with a pattern that might have been cream-colored flowers. Julia—Mrs. Pickett—owns just such a dress."

And she was wearing it with increasing frequency, he recalled, as she'd been obliged to pack away several of her dresses until after the birth, the cut of their narrow skirts not allowing for the increasing bulge of her abdomen. She would never have been so careless with it as to allow it to be caught in the carriage door—unless, of course, she was unable to prevent it, being unconscious or . . . worse. His brain shied away from the thought. Unfortunately, it seemed to be shying away from every other thought, too. He ought to be doing something, but he couldn't think what—something more than sitting here drinking something that tasted like ditchwater, in any case. He needed a plan; why couldn't he *think?* There was something he needed to tell Carson to do; what was it? Something involving newspapers . . .

"Carson, I need you to ride to Wells," he told Harry. "Find the newspaper office—it's the *Wells Journal*—and see what you can discover about an advertisement that ran there a week ago, asking for someone to reserve a room here for a man named Edward Gaines Brockton. Thomas"—he turned to address his valet—"pack my bags and your own. While you're at it, go ahead and pack Mr. Carson's, too. It may save us time."

Matthews cleared his throat discreetly. "Begging your pardon, Mr. Pickett, but Mr. Colquhoun gave orders that you were to leave Mr. Carson in charge of the case here."

"If Carson wants to stay here and chase after mare's nests, he's welcome to do so. But I don't think he'll find any Edward Gaines Brockton, because I believe no such person exists." He turned to Carson and addressed him a voice curiously humble for one who only moments ago seemed intent on choking the life out of him. "Besides, I—I would be obliged to you if you would come with me. I have a feeling I'm going to need all the help I can get."

Carson regarded his superior for a long moment before stretching his arm across the table. "All right, chief," he said at last, "I'm your man."

Matthews watched in some alarm as Pickett accepted the proffered handshake. "But—what am I to tell Mr. Colquhoun?"

"You may tell him that you delivered his orders—and that I respectfully declined to obey them."

Matthews had been fortifying himself with a pull from his tankard, but this declaration was enough to make him spray ale across the table. As Thomas scurried to mop up the mess, Matthews stammered, "But—but dash it, man, you can't—you could lose your position!"

"Yes. Or I could lose my wife."

Harry pushed back his chair. "If we're to be leaving Dunbury soon, then I suppose I'd better see about hiring a hack and riding to Wells. If you don't mind my asking, chief, what do you intend to do while I'm gone?"

Pickett sighed. "I'm going to pay a call on my wife's family."

* * *

As he dug through the clothespress, pushing aside the evening clothes he had reluctantly instructed Thomas to pack, Pickett couldn't help remembering the dread with which he'd contemplated the idea of dressing for dinner with Julia's parents. Now, he reflected, he would have given all he possessed to have been doing exactly that. Instead, he was dressing not for dinner, but for riding, and his destination was not the home of Julia's parents, but that of her sister. Or, more specifically, her sister's husband. Pickett needed some kind of strategy, and he didn't even know where to start. Fortunately, he knew someone with experience in planning and carrying out campaigns: Major James Pennington, late of His Majesty's 7th cavalry.

After changing his clothes, Pickett went to the stable and requested the hire of a horse, preferably one gentle enough to tolerate an inexperienced rider. It said much for his state of mind that he was utterly unmindful of the grins on the faces of the stable hands who witnessed his ungainly ascent into the saddle; as for deliberately waiting until Harry Carson had departed for Wells before putting his own lack of skill on display for his colleague's amusement, such an idea never even entered his head. Instead, he was hearing again Julia's voice . . .

My dear John! Are you truly offering to come to me on horseback? I am quite overcome!

"Oh, Julia," he murmured aloud, "I would crawl on my hands and knees, if only—"

But he would not think of that, not now. In a way, he was thankful for the need to concentrate on staying in the saddle; it gave his brain an occupation besides wondering where Julia was, and whether she was safe and unharmed. Or whether she was alive at all.

In such a manner the miles went by, and he passed through the gates of the estate called Greenwillows just as the sun was beginning to set. He left his hack in the care of the groomsman who came to meet him, then walked as one in a daze to the front door of the house, where he asked for a word with Major Pennington.

"I'm afraid he and Mrs. Pennington are presently at

dinner," the butler said, clearly prepared to close the door on him. "If you would care to leave your card, however—"

"Please—it's an emergency," Pickett insisted, discreetly planting his foot just inside the door, in case the butler was not convinced.

"And who shall I say is calling?" the butler inquired.

"John Pickett, of—" He broke off just before saying *of Bow Street* from sheer force of habit. "—of London," he said instead, adding, "I'm Mrs. Pennington's brother by marriage."

"Very good, sir."

The butler left him in the foyer, and returned a moment later. "If you will follow me, sir?"

Pickett did, and was led up a flight of stairs and down the corridor. They passed the stately formal dining room on the left, with its enormous painting over the fireplace and the long mahogany table that seated twenty, and turned instead into a much smaller room fitted out for intimate family dining. Pickett noticed that, while Jamie Pennington sat at the head of the table, his wife, Claudia, had rejected her rightful place at its foot in order to sit beside her husband instead—the same seating arrangement, in fact, that prevailed at his and Julia's home in Curzon Street. *Julia . . .*

"Why, Mr. Pickett, what a pleasant surprise!" exclaimed Claudia, looking up from her plate. "But I must remember to call you John, mustn't I? Tell me, have you eaten? Morris, pray fetch another plate—"

"No, no," Pickett said hastily, his stomach roiling at the idea of eating anything at such a time. "I just came to—I need your help—"

"What's wrong?" Jamie asked, frowning.

"It's Julia." He swallowed hard. "She's been abducted."

For the second time that day—had it really been only a few hours? It seemed an eternity!—Pickett recounted the details of Andrew's sworn statement.

"Why, it's wicked!" cried Claudia, horrified. "Who would do such a thing?"

"I should rather ask 'why' would anyone do such a thing," her husband said thoughtfully. "If you could determine 'why,' you would very likely know 'who.' "

Pickett turned gratefully to his brother-in-law, who, just as he'd hoped, appeared to have a clear head and a firm grasp on the situation, insofar as it had been revealed to him. "I think—that is, I'm certain I know."

"You know why, or who?"

"Both. And I swear to God it was an accident, but I couldn't make him believe it." It all came pouring out then, things he had never told to anyone but his magistrate: the Lake District and the confrontation that had taken place there; the distraction provided by Julia's arrival and the ensuing struggle for the pistol; the loud report and the woman's face, frozen in an expression of surprise that might have been comical, had it not been for the bright red stain spreading across the front of her gown; and, finally, the threat that still caused Pickett to awaken drenched with fear and sweat in the middle of the night. *You have a wife there, one you love…Shall I do to her what you did to mine?… No, not today, but someday, someday when you're least expecting it, when you've convinced yourself that it's safe to lower your guard…*

"And with such a threat hanging over her head, what must Julia do but decide to host a tea party! How could she be so thoughtless of her own safety?" Claudia pushed back her chair and began pacing about the room in mingled fear and frustration. "Surely she must have known—"

"She didn't."

Claudia paused in her pacing and blinked at him in confusion. "I beg your pardon?"

"She didn't know she was in any danger," Pickett confessed miserably. "I didn't tell her."

"You *what?*" As bewilderment gave way to belligerence, her face—the face so similar to Julia's—turned crimson with fury.

"I—I didn't want her to worry," he said in his own defense. And while this had seemed like a reasonable course of action at the time, it now sounded like the feeblest of excuses, even to his own ears. "I mean—her condition—the baby—"

"How *dare* you? How dare you use her condition as an excuse for keeping her in ignorance? You might at least have allowed her the agency of deciding for herself whether to worry or not!"

There was nothing, not one word, that he could offer as a rebuttal. Perhaps that was why Jamie chose to do it for him. "Don't be so hard on him, Claudia. I daresay I would have done the same thing at his age."

"Yes, I daresay you would have," she agreed bitterly. "Tell me, do young men have to work at being stupid, or does it come naturally?"

Jamie's voice hardened. "I know you're frightened for her, Claudia—so am I—but no purpose can be served by casting blame. Besides, it seems to me that you, of all people, have no cause to question John's intelligence. If it weren't for him, you would very likely still be married to his lordship, and hiding on the Peninsula."

Pickett wasn't sure which he found the most objectionable: being talked about as if he were still in the schoolroom (not that he'd ever actually spent that much time there) or being talked about as if he weren't even present. But however unsatisfying he found the conversation, he could not argue with its results. Immediately, the fire went out of Claudia, and she came to him with outstretched arms.

"Jamie is right. I'm being horrid to you, and I'm so sorry." She enfolded him in an embrace and, after a moment's awkwardness, he returned it, savoring the contact with another human being, united by their mutual love for Julia and fear for her safety. "It's only that I just got my sister back; I can't bear to think of losing her again."

On that much, they were agreed. Pickett might have told her so, but the little *tête-à-tête* was interrupted by Jamie. "There's a moon tonight, so we need not wait until morning to start out—assuming, of course, that you have some idea of where we should begin to look for her."

"The Lake District," Pickett said without hesitation. "A village called Banfell. But first we have to go back to the Cock and Boar in Dunbury. I have a colleague from the Horse Patrol—I sent him on an errand to Wells, but he should have returned by the time we get there. My valet is there as well, packing our bags."

"And while Jamie is upstairs packing his own bag," Claudia spoke up firmly, "you, my brother John, are going to sit down and eat."

Pickett shook his head. "I couldn't possibly eat anything—"

"Nonsense! You can be of no use to Julia if you're fainting from hunger before you ever reach her."

Pickett could not argue with the truth of this statement, but neither could he taste anything of the very respectable repast cobbled together from his sister- and brother-in-law's leavings. He contrived to swallow enough to stave off the demands of his stomach, and by the time he had finished picking at a treacle tart that at any other time he would have put away with considerable relish, Jamie had returned to the small dining room, his greatcoat thrown over his riding clothes and a bulging valise in his hand.

"Are you ready, then?" he asked, observing Pickett's empty plate. "Good! Let's be on our way."

Claudia followed them downstairs as far as the front door, where she bade her husband a fond farewell before saying, "I won't ask to go with you, for I know I would only slow you down. Still, if there anything I can do here—"

"Actually, there is," Pickett confessed. "I would be obliged to you if you would break the news to your parents."

She considered this request for a moment before agreeing to it, with one caveat. "I shall tell Mama and Papa everything they need to know, but I don't think I shall tell them anything just yet." She stood on tiptoe to kiss him on the cheek, then added tremulously, "She'll be all right, you know. How can she not, when the two cleverest and best men in England are coming to her rescue?"

10

In Which Plans Are Made for Julia's Rescue

T hey left the house and walked to the stables, where, to Pickett's surprise, Jamie didn't order his horse to be saddled, but the traveling chaise to be prepared instead. As the groom led the carriage horses from their stalls, Jamie hefted his valise onto the boot and strapped it securely in place.

"I—I hired a hack," Pickett was moved to protest, although not without a pang of regret at the thought of giving up a place inside a well-sprung chaise to pick his way instead along the road on horseback, with no more light than that provided by the waning gibbous moon.

"I'll hitch your mount to the back of the carriage," Jamie said. "Mind you, I'll have to send the carriage back, if not tonight, then first thing in the morning—I won't leave Claudia with no means of transportation—but we can hire a post-chaise."

"I should have thought you would prefer to ride," Pickett protested feebly.

"Ordinarily, I would, and I daresay your man from the Horse Patrol would, too, but I expect you'll find it much more comfortable to be driven." Seeing the play of emotions that flitted across Pickett's expressive countenance, he added, "Yes, I know you want to save face, but there's no shame in owning one's limitations. I suspect we'll want to travel at a brisker pace than you would be comfortable with on horseback, and when we find Julia, we'll need a carriage to bring her back in."

Pickett's brow cleared at his use of "when" rather than "if." "Yes—of course—I hadn't thought—" He shook his head as if to clear it. "Truth to tell, I can't seem to think of anything much."

And that, Jamie reflected, was hardly surprising, under the circumstances. He was not at all so confident of their victorious outcome as he had allowed his brother-in-law to believe, but he had no more intention of divulging his doubts than he had of allowing Pickett, in his present state of mind, to occupy the carriage alone, where his darkest thoughts might prey upon him. It was the sort of reasoning that had made him an excellent officer, and that would have made him an excellent vicar, had his elopement with the very married Claudia, Lady Buckleigh, not put paid to that particular career path.

"Better still," Pickett added thoughtfully, "perhaps we ought to hire a vehicle that we can drive ourselves. We could take the driving in turns, and travel through the night."

"Think, man!" Jamie chided him. "You're talking about a journey of three hundred miles. Even if we drove straight through, stopping only to eat and change horses, we'd be dead on our feet by the time we reached Banfell. From what you've said, this fellow we're after is a crafty one. We'll need to be awake and alert if we hope to best him."

This description aligned perfectly with Pickett's recollections of the man. Still, every minute they delayed was one more minute that Julia was at the mercy of a madman, suffering who knew what horrors. The expression on his face must have told its own tale, for Jamie clapped a hand to his shoulder and gave it an encouraging squeeze, then a shake.

"I know, old boy," he said. "But you've got to buck up, for her sake. It'll do her no good at all if we go off half-cocked with no sleep and no plan as to what we're going to do when we get there." He turned to address his groom. "Are you ready there, Kirby? Good! Let's be off."

He gave Pickett one last, brisk clap on the back, then nudged him toward the carriage door before climbing in after him. Kirby scrambled up onto the box, and the search for Julia was officially underway.

Darkness had fallen by the time they reached the Cock and Boar. Just as Pickett had predicted, Carson had returned from his errand in Wells, and lost no time in informing his superior of his findings.

"You may be onto something, chief," he told Pickett, after he and Thomas had been presented to Major Pennington. "About there being no such person as Edward Gaines Brockton, I mean. It turns out that the advertisement wasn't placed by him at all, but by someone named James Sullivan."

"That means something to you?" Jamie asked, seeing

Pickett's gaze sharpen.

"I've seen it before," Pickett said. "On a letter found in the coat pocket of a dying man." As he recalled, that letter had also included Sullivan's direction. He cast about in his memory for it. "He's in Dublin, or at least, he was. Mountjoy Square, to be exact."

"What do you think, then?" Jamie asked. "Should we go there, instead of Banfell?"

Pickett considered the matter. "I think Robert Hetherington is too clever a man to return to his estate near Banfell. He knows that's the first place he'd be looked for."

Carson frowned. "I thought you said the fellow was mad."

"As a March hare," Pickett said bluntly. "But that doesn't mean he can't be cunning."

"But why Dublin? He isn't Irish, is he?"

"No, but his wife is—was." Again Pickett recalled the gunshot, and the expression on the man's face when he realized his wife had been hit. In a way, he could understand Hetherington's determination to hold him to blame: the truth—that he himself had killed his beloved wife—was too terrible for him to contemplate. Looking back, Pickett suspected Hetherington's sanity had been hanging by a thread for decades before her death had finally pushed him over the edge. Pickett doubted that a few weeks in prison had done anything to restore his mind. "She'd been—mistreated—by the English after her father took part in an uprising in the last century. The English army," he added as an aside to Jamie, "so it's a good thing you're no longer in uniform."

"Begging your pardon, sir," put in Thomas, who up to this point had listened in slack-jawed silence, "but it don't seem to make much difference."

"There you have me," Pickett conceded. "But her family had an estate somewhere in Ireland. It would have become forfeit to the Crown once her father was convicted of treason, but if it's still standing empty, it might make a convenient bolt-hole for anyone hiding from the law."

"Do you know where it is?" Jamie asked.

Pickett shook his head. "No idea. I suppose it must be somewhere near Carrickfergus, since that's where the uprising took place, but beyond that—" He broke off, shrugging.

"*You* might not know, but someone in Mountjoy Square might," declared Jamie, pushing back his chair. "If we leave now, we should be able to reach Bristol by midnight. We can get an early start tomorrow and reach Holyhead in two days, then take the packet across the channel to Dublin."

"*Two days?*" echoed Pickett, white-faced and desperate. "Anything could have happened to her in that time!"

"I'm afraid it can't be helped," Jamie said, albeit not without sympathy. "I suppose we might try to hire a boat in Bristol—provided the seas are not too rough, travel over water might be swifter than making the same journey over land—but anyone with a craft capable of making the trip would almost certainly require payment up front, and I don't have sufficient money on me at present."

This observation led, not unnaturally, to all four men emptying their pockets and dumping the contents of their coin purses out onto the table. Granted, Pickett was no sailor; his one venture out to sea in a fishing boat off the coast of Scotland had ended with his losing his breakfast into the Irish Sea. Still, if he could reach Julia even one minute sooner via water than might be accomplished over land, he would consider it well worth any discomfort. But when their communal bank was tallied, the general consensus was that, although they might find a sailor sufficiently needful of funds to take them to Dublin for such a sum, it would be foolhardy in the extreme to be decanted upon the docks of Dublin without so much as a farthing left between them.

"Once we reach Bristol, we'll stop at the nearest posting-house and ask if they have two rooms vacant," Jamie said, his mind already leaping ahead to meet the next obstacle. "We may have to make shift with one, but if not, John and I will share one, and Carson and Thomas can take the other."

Thomas looked up at the mention of his name. "But I thought I would be putting up with the stable hands, like I am here."

"We can get in and out much more quickly if we're all together—under the same roof, if not in the same room."

"Looks like you just got promoted," Carson told the valet. He raised his tankard in a toast. "Or conscripted, I'm not sure which. Either way, we're all a part of Major Pennington's irregulars."

"Not mine," Jamie protested, lifting his tankard all the same. "Gentlemen, I give you Pickett's Irregulars."

"Pickett's Irregulars," chorused the others, and succeeded in dragging a shadow of a smile from the little band's namesake. If he had to endure this waking nightmare, at least he had men around him whom he could trust.

Having determined on a course of action, Pickett dispatched Thomas upstairs to fetch their bags while he settled up with the Cock and Boar. Nancy was much inclined to bemoan the loss of her swain, but upon being commanded by Jamie (whom she mentally dismissed as an unfeeling brute without a romantic bone in his body) to cease caterwauling, she kissed Harry goodbye and left her post long enough to step outside, where she stood waving her handkerchief at the departing carriage until it disappeared around the bend.

* * *

The hours that followed seemed to Pickett like a nightmare from which he could not awaken. The lamps mounted on the outside of the post-chaise only served to make the darkness beyond seem even darker by comparison, meaning he could find no distraction in the unfamiliar scenery they passed along the way. About an hour into their journey, Carson conceived the happy notion of whiling away the time in singing, at the top of his lungs (or so it seemed to Pickett), a selection of bawdy tunes of the sort most frequently heard in London's less discriminating public houses. He was possessed of a fine, if untrained, tenor voice, to which Thomas very readily contributed his own baritone. Jamie soon added his own voice to the mix, and finally, Pickett himself joined in, albeit halfheartedly; it was easier than resisting Carson's constant urging, or deflecting his insistence that there was, after all, nothing Pickett could do for his wife at the moment— a fact of which he was all too painfully aware. To his surprise, it actually helped, as much as anything could; it was, after all, difficult to form horrifying theories as to what torments Julia might be suffering when he was trying to recall the words to the next stanza of "The Jug of Punch" or "Drink Old England Dry."

At last they reached Bristol and soon located a posting-house, where Jamie sent his companions inside to procure a couple of rooms while he gave instructions for a vehicle and fresh horses to be ready for their departure at dawn the following morning. It was quite late by this time, and the innkeeper was not pleased to be rousted from his bed at such an hour, but was forced to comply nonetheless; unlike the village of Dunbury with its one inn, Bristol was a city of considerable size, and if he were disinclined to oblige the latecomers, they would have no difficulty in locating a more welcoming establishment.

Entering the quiet chamber which he was to share his brother-in-law, Pickett noted that it appeared to be clean, and was somewhat roomier than the lodgings provided by the Cock and Boar. Not that it appeared to matter much to Jamie either way, Pickett noticed with a pang of envy; having spent more than a dozen years in the army, the major had acquired the ability to sleep anywhere. Soon the stillness was interrupted only by the rhythmic sounds of his breathing.

Alas, with nothing else to distract him, the demons Pickett had previously held at bay came rushing back to torment him. But now, instead of wondering where Julia was at that moment and what was happening to her, his thoughts drifted back to the last night before he'd left for Dunbury, and their farewells at dawn the following morning. She'd teased him about making her a formal offer of marriage, but he could tell that she was speaking only half in jest. Why hadn't he done it? Partly—mostly, perhaps—because he didn't know how to put in words the depth of his love for her. But surely she would have recognized his dilemma, and given him credit for trying. It would have made her happy, and would have cost him nothing. Oh, he might have felt a little foolish, going down on one knee to offer marriage to a woman who was already his wife—a lady, moreover, who was already four months gone with his child—but there would have been no one else to see. Even if there had been, if Rogers or Thomas had entered the room unexpectedly and caught him in the act, well, it wasn't as if he'd never made a fool of himself before.

He might have missed that opportunity to please her, but there was another awaiting him in London. He could accept the position offered by the Prince of Wales. Granted, he did not look forward to the loss of autonomy the position would entail, but surely restoring Julia to something approaching the station in life that should have been hers would make the sacrifice worthwhile. At least, he reasoned, it was unlikely that anyone would be able enter Carlton House and snatch her away; he supposed it would constitute part of his duty to the prince to see that the royal residence was secure. Surely the peace of mind would more than compensate for whatever indignities he might suffer.

Oh Julia, he thought, shifting to find a better position in which to entice the sleep he knew would not come, *just be safe and unharmed, and anything you want is yours.*

11

In Which Julia Makes Plans of Her Own

J ulia shifted, vaguely conscious that the mattress beneath her was much firmer than it should have been. She stretched out an arm to ascertain from her husband if he were aware of this curious circumstance, or if (as was more likely the case) he had already arisen and departed for Bow Street. Her hand met only smooth wood, lightly dusted with a gritty layer of dirt. As her brain struggled to make sense of this discovery, she realized that the hard surface beneath her was not stationary, but shuddered with the bouncing, lurching movements of a poorly-sprung carriage.

She was not in bed at all, then, but in a moving carriage. But why was she lying on the floor, instead of sitting on the seat? She opened her eyes, and found herself staring at the scuffed toes of a pair of boots so close to her face that to focus her gaze upon them rendered her cross-eyed. She had not realized her husband's footwear was in such shabby condition; she would urge him to see Hoby about measuring

137

him for new ones. Although, she reflected, rubbing a sore spot on the back of her head, any man so ungallant as to allow his wife to tumble off the seat without lifting a finger to stop her no doubt deserved to go about with holes in the toe. And so she would tell him, the moment they reached—wherever it was they were going. She couldn't remember.

"Ah, so you're awake then, are you?"

The voice, though friendly enough, was definitely *not* that of her husband. John's speech comprised a veneer of gentility carefully spread over the Cockney vowels of his youth, which still had a tendency to manifest themselves in times of great emotion. This voice, though less genteel than John's best efforts, was nevertheless soft and lilting, almost musical. And yet the sound of it filled her with a nameless dread. *Why?*

She turned her head in order to look up at the speaker. A man sat on the rear-facing seat, a man of about thirty with ginger hair and bright blue eyes. His green tailcoat, plum-colored waistcoat, and buff breeches were shabby imitations of the current fashion, and on the seat beside him lay a stout wooden cudgel. At the sight of it, her memory came rushing back: the disastrous tea party; Rogers lying insensible on the floor as blood trickled down his hair and onto the polished marble; and this man, standing over her fallen butler with this same weapon in his hand . . .

"Who are you?" she demanded, trying her best to sound indignant rather than terrified. "Where are you taking me?"

"I'll be tellin' you all in good time, Mrs. Pickett. In the meantime, I don't doubt you'll feel much more comfortable in the seat. If you'll allow me?"

He offered his hand, but Julia was not inclined to take it. Instead, she pushed herself upright to a sitting position, then braced her hands on the edge of the forward-facing seat and climbed onto it.

"Your voice," she said, placing it with some surprise. "You're Irish."

"Aye, that I am," he said, sounding gratified. "Born and bred there. *Éire go Brách*," he added, and it seemed to Julia that there was an edge to his voice that had not been there before.

She was almost certain that she'd heard the phrase before, but she could not recall where, or in what context. In fact, she could think of only two acquaintances who hailed from the land which the poet William Drennan had dubbed "the Emerald Isle": a charming albeit impoverished young man whom she had once considered taking as a lover, since it had appeared at the time that she could never have the man she truly wanted—good heavens! What *had* she been thinking?—and an older woman, recently deceased.

"What does it mean?" she asked, her brow puckered as she tried to think under what circumstances either one of these acquaintances might have uttered the phrase. "The words you just spoke, that is."

" 'Ireland forever' captures the meanin', although 'Ireland to eternity' is perhaps a more literal translation of the Gaelic. It is the heartfelt cry of all those who crave Irish independence from Britain—aye, crave it to the point that we're willin' to fight, even to die, in order to achieve it."

"Is that what this is all about, then?" Julia asked. Any sense of relief she might have felt at this explanation was quickly overwhelmed by an equal portion of despair: however valid their grievances against the English, she put the likelihood of the Crown's agreeing to grant Ireland its independence somewhere between slim and none. Her captor might be less than pleased by this statement of fact; what, then, might he do to her in an effort to assuage his disappointment? "If that is the case, then I fear you have made a tactical error. It is true that my first husband was a person of some importance at Court, but any influence I might once have exerted has died with him. I'm afraid there is nothing I can do to aid your cause."

She had spoken in cosseting tones, but these apparently fell on deaf ears.

"I think you underestimate yourself, Mrs. Pickett," her captor assured her. "We—my compatriots and I—don't expect you to work miracles. My purpose in takin' you from your home is not to procure Irish independence—at least, not directly—but to assist one of our number in avengin' an old wrong. He is not an Irishman himself, you understand, but he supports our cause out of devotion to his Irish wife."

"Oh?" His words stirred a chord of memory, but the situation he seemed to suggest was impossible—wasn't it?

"Oh, aye. As a young lass, she was mistreated by a group of English soldiers—I'll be sparin' you the details, as they're not fit for a lady's ears."

"I see," she said slowly. "One hears of such things, although they are abhorrent to any person of feeling, no matter the nationality of the perpetrators or their unfortunate victim. Still, if you are speaking of the man I think you are, I can't understand what you hope to gain by abducting me. The event you describe took place before I was ever born, and the lady herself is dead—may she rest in peace," Julia added in an effort to soften the blunt statement.

"Aye, she's dead—at the hands of an Englishman, who shot her in cold blood."

"I fear you have been misinformed, Mr.—" Too late, she realized she didn't know the man's name. As he made no effort to enlighten her ignorance, she was obliged to continue without it. "It is true that she was shot, but her death was a— a tragic accident, the result of two men fighting for possession of the same weapon. Furthermore, the man for whom you are attempting to seek vengeance is in prison."

The man on the seat opposite shook his head. "Much as it pains me to contradict a lady, I'm obliged to say that he's no such thing."

"He—he's *not* in prison, you say?" She wished her head didn't ache so. The pain made it difficult to think, and she had a feeling she would need all her faculties to function at peak capacity if she hoped to extricate herself from her present dilemma. "But he was found guilty of high treason!"

"One man's treason is another man's patriotism," her captor observed, and although he gave a careless shrug, Julia was once again aware of the hint of steel underlying his words. "I'll not be denyin' that he was convicted at the Carlisle assizes, but my countrymen and I were able to save him."

"You helped him to escape." Somehow saying the words

aloud made them sound more real, and more terrifying.

"As you say," he agreed, inclining his head. "And only just in time. They would be after stretchin' his neck the very next day. A week ago, that was."

"And where has he gone to ground in the meantime? Not to his estate in the Lake District, surely?"

"Ah, but that would be tellin'." He winked at her, as if they were discussing nothing more than a prank by a mischievous child. "Suffice it to say you'll be findin' out soon enough."

And that, Julia reflected, was exactly what she was afraid of.

* * *

Julia could not tell how long she had been insensible on the carriage floor, and thus had no way of knowing how long they had been on the road, or how far they had traveled. Nor did she have any very clear idea of where they were, although by tracing the sun's path across the sky, she had determined that they were heading roughly northwestward; it appeared they were headed for the Lake District, after all. And when they reached it—what then?

She was not inclined to linger in this ruffian's company long enough to find out. At one point, she noticed his eyes had drooped closed and his head lolled back against the wall of the carriage. Did she dare open the door and jump? She had leaped from a moving carriage once before; granted, on that occasion the vehicle had not yet left the yard of the posting-house, and therefore was traveling at a much slower rate of speed. Then, too, John had been present to catch her. There would be no one to do so this time, and no way to break her fall. She had no doubt her captor could outrun her, so she would have only as much time to make good her escape as it took for him to realize she was gone and order the driver to bring the carriage to a stop. There was a farmhouse some distance ahead on the left, where she might be able to plead for help. Perhaps if she were to make her move just as they drew abreast of it . . .

She eased herself forward onto the edge of the seat, then reached for the door handle. One . . . two . . .

She glanced at the man seated opposite. He had not moved a muscle, but his eyes were open, watching.

She let out a long breath, released her grip on the door handle, and sank back on the seat.

"Very wise of you, Mrs. Pickett," said her captor, and closed his eyes again.

Julia, however daunted, was not yet defeated. Even the most determined abductor must eventually call a halt, however brief, to change horses, or to partake of a meal, or simply to answer the call of nature. Until then, she resolved to bide her time.

* * *

After what seemed an eternity, Julia felt the movement of the carriage begin to slow, and a moment later they turned off the road and into the bustling yard of an inn. As it lurched to a stop, she rose somewhat stiffly from her seat. Immediately, her companion stretched out his leg to block her access to the door.

"And just where might you be goin'?" he asked, and

although his voice was pleasant enough, there was an undeniable menace undergirding it.

"I need to visit the necessary," she informed him. "Unless you wish to clean up after me, I suggest you let me."

Julia was almost certain that his lips twitched, but any illusions she might have entertained that he might be won over through humor died in the next instant. He leaped down from the carriage and held out his hand to help her alight. But as soon as her feet touched the ground, his grip on her arm tightened painfully.

"No tricks, Mrs. P., or it'll be very much the worse for you."

To her dismay, he did not release her, but led her into the inn and bespoke dinner for the two of them, along with a private parlor where they might partake of it. Clearly, there would be no appealing to any of their fellow guests for assistance in making her escape. As for the necessary, he inquired as to the location of this facility, then, upon being given an answer, inquired of their host as to whether he had a wife or daughter who might come to her assistance.

"Pretty as a mornin' in May, my wife is, but quite mad," he added, lowering his voice to a conspiratorial whisper. "Seems to have the idea that I'm carryin' her off against her will."

"It's true," she insisted to the innkeeper's wife as soon as the two women were alone. "He *is* carrying me off against my will!"

"Now, now," the woman spoke soothingly, "I'm sure I can recognize a runaway match when I see one. Never you mind, dearie, it's only natural-like to be having second thoughts. That don't mean you're mad, though, not by a long chalk—and so I shall tell that man of yours! But never you mind; once the pair of you is leg-shackled, you'll be merry as a grig, and wondering how you could ever have doubted your man."

"He's not 'my man'! He's a complete stranger!"

"They all are, dearie," said the innkeeper's wife, nodding sagely. "It's my opinion that no woman really knows her man until they've lived together as man and wife."

"I don't even know his name!"

At last Julia succeeded in provoking a reaction, albeit not the one she had hoped for. The woman began to laugh so heartily that both her chins were set aquiver. "Lud, the pair of you were in a powerful hurry, weren't you? Still, if you was ready to elope on no more acquaintance than that—"

"We are *not* eloping! I tell you, I'm being abducted!" Julia insisted, but she might have saved her breath. The innkeeper's wife was sentimental by nature, but in the years since she'd reared no fewer than five daughters to adulthood and seen them all suitably wed, romance had been sadly missing from her own life. In its absence, she had cast Julia in her mind as a runaway bride who, having successfully eloped with her swain, now regarded with fear and trembling the imminent surrender of her maidenhood. Nothing Julia could say or do had the power to dispel this pleasing image.

"Here's your lady again, right as a trivet," she sang out as they rejoined Julia's captor in the private parlor. Leaning over the back of his chair, she added in a stage whisper, "You be gentle with her, now, d'ye hear? The poor dearie's skittish as a fawn. But I can see I don't have to tell you what to do, for anyone can see you're that devoted to her, you can hardly bear to let her out of your sight. Reminds me of when Himself and me was a-courtin'," she added with a wistful sigh, turning away to let them enjoy their dinner in privacy.

"Wait!" Julia cried, trying another tactic. "If a man should come asking for me—a man named John Pickett—tell him—" Tell him what? She had no idea where she was or where she was being taken. Nor, for that matter, did she know the name of her abductor, or what he hoped to accomplish by abducting her.

"Never you mind." The woman turned back to give her what Julia supposed was intended as a reassuring smile. "I'll know just how to deal with your father, if he wants to come poking his nose in where it's not wanted."

"He's not my—"

But it was too late. Her hostess was already waddling away, and her captor pushed back his chair and rose from the table, ready to hustle her back into the carriage, dinner or no. Clearly, he did not intend to take the chance that she might yet persuade someone—anyone!—that she was being taken against her will. She might have pointed out to him that the likelihood of anyone believing such a tale was small; even the most sympathetic of listeners would press her for details as to why she was being taken, and where, and Julia could offer none. Perhaps her next move should be to determine what she could about where he was taking her and just what were his plans for her when they arrived there. Exactly what she might do with this information once she procured it, she didn't know; still, it must be to her advantage to form some kind of plan, even an incomplete one.

"And so," she observed aloud, once they were back on the road, "Mr. Hetherington has escaped from prison with your assistance, in exchange for his promise that he will aid you in the cause of Irish independence if you will—what? Kill me? But you might have done that in London, with far less trouble to yourself."

Silence was the only response she received.

"Unless," she continued, undaunted, "he doesn't trust you not to be persuaded by my *beaux yeux* into taking pity on me, and intends to do the thing himself."

Evidently the suggestion that he might be untrustworthy (or more susceptible to feminine wiles than he might care to admit) had the effect of loosening his tongue. "He trusts me," he said, bristling. "He trusts me to bring you to him safe and unharmed."

" 'Unharmed'? What a pity you didn't remember that bit before coshing me on the head," she retorted, massaging the sore spot on her scalp.

"Aye, he won't be best pleased about that, but it was the only way to get you into the carriage."

"Yes, I suppose I'm quite unreasonable about being abducted from my home in broad daylight. I daresay I should beg your pardon for putting you to so much trouble, but I find myself quite unable to do so. Still, I can't quite see why our mutual friend insists that I be 'safe and unharmed' if he intends to kill me anyway."

"Oh, it's not you he's after. You're only the bait by which he means to reel in your husband."

"In that case, I fear you have both made a rather important mistake. My husband is in Dunbury." It seemed oddly dreamlike, she thought, to be discussing the details of her own capture and, presumably, eventual murder. She could imagine herself awakening shortly and recounting the details to her husband over the breakfast table, where they would both laugh over the absurdity of it all. At least, she would have laughed. But in retrospect, she realized that John's demeanor had been devoid of laughter in the weeks since they had returned from the Lake District. His was not a giddy nature, and so she had not noticed until now. Had he imagined that something like this might happen? If so, then why had he not confided in her?

The Irishman's next words quickly drove the question from her mind. "To be sure, he's in Dunbury. Who do you think sent him there?"

"*You?*"

He shrugged. "The letter was written by our mutual friend, but I was the one entrusted with seein' it posted."

"But—but it was signed 'Edward Gaines Brockton'!"

Again that careless shrug, as if they were discussing of no more importance than the weather. "Edward Gaines Brockton—E.G.B.—*Éire go Brách*." Seeing her momentarily bereft of speech, he added, "It was necessary, you see, to get Mr. Pickett out of London for a few days, and with a colleague in tow, just to make sure he couldn't bring you along as he did to the Lake District. Now it's just a matter of seein' how long it takes him to discover he's been sent on a chase after mare's nests."

And just that quickly, her absurd "dream" had turned to nightmare. This abduction was not really about her at all; no, it was a carefully planned and painstakingly executed plot for vengeance against one who had done nothing to deserve it.

"Tell me," she said slowly, trying her best to keep her voice from shaking, "did you kill my butler?"

He waved one hand in a gesture of contempt. "Pshaw! Of course not! I daresay the fellow had come 'round before we reached Hyde Park."

And once conscious, Rogers would have lost no time in sending Andrew to Bow Street, she deduced. Would Mr. Colquhoun have sent word to John in Dunbury, or would he have dispatched whatever Runner happened to be nearest to hand, in the hope of overtaking them on the road? She hoped it was the latter—a set of pretty fools her captors would look, if the wrong fish took the bait!—but she feared the former were far more likely. The bond between her husband and his magistrate was deep and strong, all the more so for the necessity of pretending, at least in front of the other men under Mr. Colquhoun's supervision, that it did not exist. She had no doubt that Mr. Colquhoun would send his swiftest courier to Dunbury with the news. And after John came in pursuit, then—what?

If her abduction—and, presumably, her death—were to be Mr. Hetherington's revenge, then it behooved her to consider exactly what form that vengeance might take. She tried to recall the sequence of events that had led to the death of Brigid Hetherington, but her own memories were vague. She had spoken the truth when she'd told her captor that the woman's death had not been murder, but a tragic accident; Brigid Hetherington been shot as the two men had struggled for possession of the pistol. Beyond that, however, Julia knew very little. John was mostly silent on the subject, although she suspected it still preyed on his mind a month later. It appeared, moreover, that Robert Hetherington held John responsible for the death of his wife, even though he'd held the gun in his own hand. Did he think to force John to witness her own murder before being killed himself? Perhaps crueler still, did he intend to compel John do the deed with his own hands, and then leave him to live with the consequences of his guilt?

Either way, one thing was certain: this time she must rescue herself, rather than wait for husband to do so. For both of them would be safe only as long as he stayed in Dunbury, or London—or anywhere, really, so long as it was far, far away.

12

*In Which John Pickett Receives
a Most Unwelcome Gift*

P ickett and his Irregulars, as Harry Carson had dubbed the
little group, arose at dawn the next morning and
prepared for their first full day on the road. The post-chaise
Jamie had ordered drew up into the inn yard as Pickett was
attempting, without much success, to choke down a bowl of
porridge. The arrival of this vehicle appeared to relieve him
of the necessity of completing this task, and so he pushed the
bowl away with no small sense of relief.

"Thomas, Carson," Jamie called, addressing them as if
he were still a cavalry officer and they two of the soldiers
under his command, "see to the stowing of our bags while I
settle our tab here. You"—he turned his attention to Pickett,
who had risen from the table—"sit back down and finish that."

"I couldn't—"

"You can, and you will," Jamie said in a voice that
brooked no argument.

"I want to be on the road," Pickett insisted. "God only knows what may be happening to Julia, while I sit here eating breakfast!" He glared at the bowl as if its very existence offended him.

"Very well, then." Jamie snatched the porridge off the table and disappeared from the room. Pickett felt somewhat deflated; he hadn't expected his brother-in-law to yield so quickly. But the reason for Jamie's strategic retreat became clear a few minutes later, when he returned bearing a brown earthenware bowl with a large chip out of its rim.

"I gave the cook tuppence for the oldest container she had, so you can take it with you and eat it on the way."

Pickett peered inside and discovered not only the remains of his own breakfast, but, he suspected, a couple more ladlesful for good measure. "I don't doubt you mean well, but—"

"But me no buts, brother mine. You invited me on this little jaunt, and I refuse to deliver you over to Julia looking like a scarecrow."

Jamie's calm assumption that it was merely a matter of time before they found Julia safe and sound had the desired effect, although Pickett had to wonder if his brother-in-law actually believed it, or was merely putting on a good show for his sake. In the end, he decided it was better not to know; he would take whatever reassurances he could get.

Having finished transacting his business with the innkeeper, Jamie led Pickett outside where Carson and Thomas were already waiting, and the four men piled into the post-chaise. The Bristol Channel was at this point too wide to be forded, so they were obliged to follow it northeastward for some distance until the channel narrowed to form the River Severn. Here they stopped in Gloucester long enough to change horses and fortify themselves with a hearty repast— yet another meal for which Pickett had no appetite. In fact, he had found this first leg of the journey particularly maddening, as they were very likely farther from Julia now than they had been when they'd set out from Bristol that morning, but, as Jamie pointed out, there was no help for it, unless he intended to swim across the channel.

Once their meal was completed and fresh horses were harnessed and ready, they set out again, crossing the bridge over the River Severn and continuing northwestward. This leg of the journey, a distance of more than two hundred miles, would have been grueling even under the best conditions. And it soon became clear that the conditions under which they would be obliged to travel were far from the best. The roads became more twisting and tortuous as they turned to the north, and the landscape grew so mountainous that the tops of the peaks were hidden beneath a blanket of low-hanging clouds. At lower elevations, a fog lay over the valley, softening the countryside and giving it a blurred, oddly flattened look, like a painting executed by Turner or Constable in a particularly melancholy mood.

In fact, the scenery reminded Pickett so strongly of the Lake District that he was moved to ask of no one in particular, "Where are we?"

"Wales," was Jamie's reply.

Wales, thought Pickett, *Wales, as in 'Prince of.'* Did the prince spend much time in this part of the realm from which his current title was derived, or was the designation a mere formality? He wasn't quite sure what to hope for. On the one hand, it might make a pleasant escape from Town, provided, of course, that Julia would be allowed to accompany him; on the other, the landscape, so reminiscent of the Lake District, might serve as a constant reproach, reminding him of his sojourn there and its disastrous conclusion.

Suddenly a large, dark shape loomed up out of the fog, a shape that resolved itself, as they drew nearer, into the crenelated tower of a castle, or what was left of one. Its existence presented Pickett with a new dilemma: what if Julia was being held captive not in a genteel country house, as he'd imagined, but in a fortification such as this must once have been? If he were to be obliged to storm a citadel to rescue her, then the mission might well be doomed from the start; he feared he would make a very poor knight.

At that moment, as if in agreement with this gloomy conclusion, the skies opened and the rains descended, quickly turning the roads to meandering rivers of mud and reducing visibility to such an extent that they were obliged to stop for the night fully thirty miles short of where they had intended. A pale sun greeted them the next morning, although the rains had left their mark in the form of the mud that sucked at the carriage wheels and left deep ruts that marked where other carriages had fought the same battle before them. As a result, their progress was not much swifter than it had been the day before. A rough, albeit mercifully brief sea crossing landed them on the island of Anglesey, where their first order of business was locating a post-office where they might hire a chaise to replace the one they'd been obliged to leave behind on the mainland. Alas, everyone they encountered seemed to speak with a thick accent of a kind rarely if ever heard in London, and one which presented a considerable barrier to communication. By the time they contrived to make their transportation needs understood sufficiently to be directed to a place where these needs might be met, they could go no farther than Holyhead, where they were obliged to cool their heels until dawn the next morning, when the next packet would sail for Dublin. Thomas, who had spent much of the journey with his nose pressed to the glass, recalled seeing a promising inn near the harbor, and so it was to this establishment that they repaired, descending weary, stiff, and sore from hours of inactivity.

While Thomas and Carson retrieved their now mud-spattered bags from the boot and Jamie walked down to the harbor to book passage for four on the packet for Dublin, Pickett went into the inn and requested two rooms. As he wrote his name in the register, he noticed the proprietress leaning across the counter for a closer look. This in itself was not unusual, for he wrote with his left hand, having stubbornly resisted, in his youth, any and all efforts to correct this aberration. He was about to some vague apology for this deviation from the accepted standards of penmanship—there were, after all, those who believed this trait to be the mark of the devil—when she spoke, and he realized it was not *how* he wrote, but *what* he wrote that had attracted her notice.

"So you're John Pickett, are you?"

Like her fellow countrymen, she spoke with an accent so thick as to be nearly incomprehensible, even to ears attuned to the many voices of London. Still, Pickett recognized his own name, and from her use of it, deduced that she had some message for him. After three days of feeling as if he were groping in the dark, any word from or about Julia could only be welcome.

"I am," he said hopefully, looking up from writing the direction of his London residence on the line provided for this information.

She ducked her head to rummage through the storage space beneath the counter. "Summat came t'other day along with a letter asking us to give you it. I'll get it now in a minute—ah! Here it is!"

"Thank you." The package was small and roughly cylindrical, and had been wrapped in heavy brown paper and tied with string. Pickett took it and walked across the room to where his companions waited. Jamie had just entered the inn, having finished his business on the harbor, while Thomas had brought in the last of the luggage and awaited his orders as to where it was to be conveyed. Carson seemed to be agitating in favor of stopping in the public room for a hot toddy with which they might fortify themselves after the discomforts of the journey.

"What's that?" Carson asked, pausing briefly in extolling the virtues of this plan.

"I don't know," Pickett said, pulling one end of the string until the knot came free. "Our hostess said it had been left for me. At least, I *think* that's what she said."

"Who would even know we were going to be here?" Thomas wondered aloud. "We sure didn't, until two days ago."

Pickett offered no opinion on the subject. He unrolled the tube of brown paper until it disgorged its contents— whereupon his expressive countenance changed color. He uttered a strangled sound, dropping the item and its wrappings to the floor as he ran from the inn.

"What—gorblimey!" Thomas exclaimed, his face assuming a greenish cast as Carson bent to retrieve the object and hold it up for their inspection.

It was just over two inches in length and, like its wrappings, roughly cylindrical in shape. Its color was a mottled gray, although at one time it had very likely been nearer to pink.

It was, in fact, a human finger.

* * *

"And someone left it for him here," Carson said thoughtfully. He lowered his voice, although it was unlikely that Pickett could hear him, having not yet returned from wherever he'd fled.

"In other words, someone knew we'd be pitching up here sooner or later," Jamie observed. "At least we know we're on the right track."

Thomas stared at him. "That's a bloody unfeeling way of looking at it! If you'll forgive me for saying so, sir," he added hastily, all too aware of having spoken disrespectfully not only to one of his betters, but to one of the mistress's nearest and dearest.

"If it were really her finger, you'd be right," Jamie told him. "But it's not. It can't be."

Seeing the major did not intend to hold his lapse against him, Thomas was emboldened to ask for an explanation. "Why not? If you don't mind my asking," he added hastily.

"Whoever this belongs to was dead before her finger was cut off. If you'll look at the end here, you'll see there's no sign of its having bled."

Thomas forced himself to lean in for a closer look. "At least"—he swallowed hard—"at least he'd already killed her before he did—this."

"It's very likely she died of natural causes—illness, perhaps, or childbirth. I tell you, this is not Julia's—Mrs. Pickett's—finger. It can't be."

"How do you know?"

"Because if Mrs. Pickett had been killed, it must have been done at least a week ago—and that's assuming she was murdered on the same day she was abducted. This woman, whoever she was"—he indicated the severed finger—"has been dead rather longer than that."

"You're sure about that?"

"I saw action on the Peninsula and in the Low Countries," Jamie said, his voice hardening with the recollection of long-suppressed memories. "Casualties can't always be buried in a timely manner. Let's just say I know what a dead body looks like at various stages of decomposition."

Thomas merely nodded, disinclined to ask for further enlightenment.

"So you're saying," Harry Carson put in, "that someone went to the trouble of digging up a woman's body, cutting off its finger, and sending it to Mr. Pickett here, knowing full well that he'd think the fellow was chopping his wife's fingers off? That takes a special kind of madness."

"Or a special kind of hate. The man behind her abduction holds Mr. Pickett responsible for the death of his own wife, and this seems to be his idea of revenge." Jamie cast a glance toward the door through which Pickett had fled. "And now, if you'll excuse me, I think I'd best see to him."

He left Carson and Thomas to the task of discovering to which rooms they had been assigned while he went outside in search of his brother-in-law. Pickett was not difficult to find; Jamie had only to follow the sobbing, snarling noises, more animal than human, emitting from around one corner of the inn. He reached the end of the building and discovered his young brother-in-law pressed against the half-timbered wall, his face buried in the curve of one arm while with the other arm he beat at the wall until his knuckles bled. A rather pungent pool at his feet represented all that remained of the porridge Jamie had compelled him to eat that morning.

"It's not hers, old thing." Jamie put a hand on his shoulder and gave it a reassuring squeeze, all the while speaking in low, soothing tones. "It's a cruel prank, but nothing more. It's not hers."

Gradually the significance of his words began to penetrate Pickett's brain. At last he turned to his brother-in-law with something akin to hope lightening his bleak expression. "You think so?"

"I *know* so." For the second time, Jamie explained his reasoning, concluding, "But the fact that he had it sent to you here, rather than, say, London, or the Lake District, would seem to suggest we're on the right track."

Pickett collected himself with an effort. "Yes—I know you're right—it's just—it's just that I feel so bloody *helpless!* Julia is in the clutches of a madman, and there's not a damned thing I can do about it!"

Jamie nodded. "I know," he said simply, and Pickett realized Major Pennington was probably the only man of his acquaintance who did, who could. For he, too, had been forced to stand by helplessly while the woman he loved was in danger. In Jamie's case, the danger had come from Claudia's own husband, a man with not only age and experience, but power, position, and even the law on his side. And yet Jamie had won in the end, and that without firing a shot: first when he'd carried off Claudia, Lady Buckleigh under her husband's nose, and again a dozen years later, when justice had finally caught up with his lordship.

"But," Jamie continued, more firmly now, "I disagree that there's nothing you can do. There is—and you're doing it. And now it seems to me that there's something else you can do."

"What?" Pickett asked eagerly.

"Come inside and get what sleep you can before we set out to sea in the morning."

If there was one form of transportation Pickett disliked even more than riding on horseback, it was setting out to sea in a boat. Still, he had no intention of trusting Julia's rescue to his companions while he waited patiently on land. He took a deep breath, then set his jaw and followed Jamie back inside.

* * *

The question of just how she was to get word to her husband was one that caused Julia considerable perturbation of spirits. Her abductor refused to leave her alone for a minute except when they stopped for the night, at which time he either locked her into her room and kept the key, or tied the handle of his own chamber door to the handle of hers—a fact she had discovered early in their journey, when she'd attempted to make her escape in the middle of the night while her captor slept.

It was not until the third night that a new and unexpected opportunity presented itself. Or perhaps it was the fourth night; the pain in her head had subsided, but there were still great chunks of time unaccounted for in her memory, so much so that she suspected the man of adding something to her food.

She could recall several stops during which meals had been obtained while the horses were changed, and she had vague memories of being taken aboard a sea-going vessel, although exactly how long the journey had taken, or in what direction they had traveled, was unclear. They had stopped once more for the night—or was it twice?—and although her head was finally clear, she had no idea where they were. As they had been traveling in a northwesterly direction, she thought it unlikely that they had crossed the Channel to France—a suspicion that was confirmed when the proprietress of the establishment inquired in English as to what she might do for them. And not just any English, Julia realized with growing certainty, but English spoken with the same lilting accent that distinguished her abductor's speech. Which meant they must be in Ireland—although exactly where in Ireland she had yet to determine. The framed prints adorning the walls offered no clues, at least not in the casual glances with which Julia was forced to be content. Nor could she hope to glean any information by eavesdropping on her fellow guests, since her captor had asked if he might hire a private parlor where they could partake of their dinner safe from any prying eyes.

If their hostess had seen anything unusual in this request, she had not let on. She had ushered them into a small room where, she assured them, they would not be disturbed, and then produced a hearty albeit humble meal of bacon and cabbage, to which she'd added a thick white sauce and a sprig of parsley. They had been sequestered in the private parlor with this repast for perhaps half an hour when the requested privacy was interrupted by a man in a caped frieze coat whose well-worn condition identified him as an actual coachman, rather than one of those sporting gentlemen who had appropriated the fashion and made it their own.

"Bohannan?" Her companion scowled. "What the devil might you be wantin'?"

The readiness with which her captor identified the newcomer gave Julia to understand that this was their driver. Until that moment, she had not given much thought to this individual; he had merely been a bulky but anonymous presence on the coachman's box, little more than a broad back and a somewhat misshapen hat pulled down low over his ears. Now, as she listened to their conversation, she realized that here at last was the opportunity she had been waiting for.

"I thought we were agreed that you were to be remainin' in the stables."

The unhappy Bohannan had removed his hat, and now twisted its brim in his hands, a gesture that went a long way toward explaining its sorry state.

"I know, and 'tis sorry I am to be after floutin' your wishes." Bohannan's voice betrayed his Irish origins just as surely as her captor's did. " 'Tis the front axle, it is."

"Broken?" A fierce scowl accompanied the single word.

"Not yet. But 'twill be a near-run thing if we expect to reach—where it is that we're goin'—without it." While his passenger considered the implications of this speech, Bohannan said, more urgently, "I know you're in a hurry, Flynn, but Himself won't be pleased if we're after havin' an accident on the road. Besides takin' us longer to get there, she could be hurt, or even killed. And then—"

"You don't have to be drawin' me a picture," interrupted her captor—Flynn, Julia thought, pleased to know he had a name, at any rate. He uttered what Julia suspected was a Gaelic oath. "I expect I'd best be havin' a look."

He pushed back his chair and rose, then looked down at her. "Before you go gettin' any ideas, Mrs. P., you should be aware that the stables offer a fine view of the front of the inn. If you think to escape, you'll have to be doin' it through the kitchens—and that would raise such a hullabaloo that we'd surely hear of it in the stables."

Julia hung her head in apparent defeat, but her brain was awhirl. She waited only long enough to hear the door close behind them before seeking out their hostess.

"I wonder if I might ask for your help," she said in hushed accents, glancing furtively over her shoulder at the door through which the two men had exited. "As you may have guessed, we—my companion and I—are a runaway couple." Julia silently blessed the proprietress of the earlier establishment where they had stopped, and took considerable satisfaction in the knowledge that, by giving the woman the idea that they were eloping, Flynn had himself provided the means by which she now might warn her real husband.

The woman's eyes narrowed in suspicion. "Aye, I was after thinkin' there was somethin' queerish about the pair o' ye."

"The three of us, actually, for his cousin is lending his aid by driving the carriage. But there can be no marriage over the anvil for us. I have a husband, you see, and I fear that he may at this very moment be pursuing us."

This much was true, so far as it went. But her hostess was clearly not pleased by the idea that she might be called upon to assist an adulterous union. "Well, now, and mayhap you ought to let him," she advised the runaway bride. "I'm sure it's not unusual for a married couple to be havin' a little spat from time to time."

"Yes, but this is nothing like that," Julia said with perfect truth. "Alas, some husbands are cruel and abusive, and in such a case, what choice does a woman have but to flee?"

"Aye, I suppose you're right about that," came the reluctant concession. "But then, what can you expect from the English? This man of yours is an Englishman, is he not?"

"He is, but Mr. Flynn, my"—she could not bring herself to call him her lover, not even to save her husband's life—"my gentleman friend is Irish."

"Flynn, you say?" the woman asked with renewed interest. "Aye, it's a good old Westmeath name! My late husband's sister was after marryin' a Flynn, although—but never you be mindin' that! You say you're wantin' my help?

"Yes! I want to write a letter to my husband, to be left here for him in case he comes in search of me. I shall urge him not to pursue us—Mr. Flynn and me, that is—as such a course of action could only cause pain."

Her hostess apparently took this claim quite literally. "D'you mean one of them might be killin' the other in a duel?" she asked, both thrilled and horrified at the prospect of such an outcome.

Julia had meant no such thing, although she didn't hesitate to embrace such a scenario, now that it had been presented to her. "Yes, should they meet, I fear it must come to that very thing."

"What will you be needin', then? Paper and ink brought up to your room, I suppose, and a quill?"

"Yes, and I would be obliged if you could bring me a cup of tea as well, and milk, sugar, and lemon to go with it. I find tea a wonderful composer when one is suffering from an agitation of spirits, don't you?"

To this the woman readily agreed, and so Julia was emboldened to continue. "I fear I must impose on you for one other favor. Mr. Flynn must know nothing of this. He—he is very jealous of my husband, you know. Heaven only knows how he may react if he discovers I am in communication with him, even for such a purpose as this."

The innkeeper's wife frowned at this, and gave it as her opinion that it sounded as if there was very little to choose between the two of them.

"I suppose it must sound that way," Julia acknowledged, then added, again with perfect sincerity, "but if you only knew the two of them, you would see that there can be no comparison."

"And what'll you be doin' with this letter, once you're after writin' it?"

Julia cast another surreptitious glance over her shoulder at the door, a gesture that was only half feigned. "I dare not bring it downstairs for fear Mr. Flynn will see. Instead, I shall drop it out the window of my chamber. Is there a kitchen maid or a stable hand you would trust to retrieve it for me?"

"I'll be doin' it my own self, ma'am," her co-conspirator vowed, placing a hand over her heart for emphasis.

"Excellent woman! I wish I could give you some token of my appreciation, but I was obliged to come away with nothing but the clothes on my back."

"I'm sure I don't wonder at it, ma'am, if your man's as brutal as you claim. But how am I to be knowin' him? What's his name? What does he look like?"

He's beautiful, Julia thought. *Beautiful, and brilliant, and brave, and if he were to be killed in an attempt to rescue me, I should die of grief.* Aloud, she merely said, "His name is John Pickett. He is quite tall, with brown eyes and brown hair that curls, and a diffident manner that makes people tend to underestimate him."

"Begging your pardon, ma'am, but the fellow you describe doesn't sound like the brute you're makin' him out to be."

"No," admitted Julia, improvising rapidly. "He is usually the sweetest and gentlest of men. It is only when he is in his cups that his temperament changes." In this she knew she did him an injustice, for on the one occasion when she had seen him the worse for drink, his conduct had still been nothing less than gentlemanly.

Something in her expression must have aroused her co-conspirator's suspicions, for the woman's eyes narrowed. "It sounds to me like you're still lovin' him, for all that."

"I daresay I shall love him until I die," she said, blinking back tears at the bitter irony that the last thing she could do for him was to blacken his character in order to save his life.

13

In Which Julia Writes a "Dear John" Letter

C loseted in her room upstairs, Julia lost no time in adding milk and sugar to the steaming cup of tea provided by her hostess. The lemon wedge that had accompanied them remained untouched, however, even as she raised the cup to her lips and took a long and satisfying pull; she had spoken no less than the truth when she had praised the beverage for its soothing qualities. She took two more sips, then set the cup aside to make room on the writing table for the paper and ink she had requested. It would not be an easy letter to write; she would have to couch her message in the words of a regretful lover, lest her co-conspirator be unable to resist the temptation to open the letter and read it. Fortunately, she had begun composing the missive in her head almost from the moment she had realized such a correspondence would be necessary, and so it did not take as long as it otherwise might have done.

My dearest John, she wrote, *I sit here with my teacup at my elbow—sugar, milk, and especially lemon, just the way I like it—contemplating our past, and my own future. Much as I love you (and always will), I cannot persist in a marriage that has brought me equal parts despair and bliss. Marriage is meant to last "till death do us part," I know, but surely you will agree with my own view, that it would be better to not waste precious time in trying to fix ours, which is long past being mended. And so I must beg you not to waste your energies in pursuit, but to give me up. To do otherwise can only bring pain to us both. Please know that although I must bid you farewell, there remains a part of my heart that will always be yours.*

Everything in her longed to close with declarations of everlasting love, but she dared go no further, lest she undo all she hoped to accomplish in writing it. And so, after signing her name with a flourish, she lifted the edge of her skirt and carefully wiped the nib clean on the hem of her petticoat, then jabbed it into the previously neglected lemon wedge.

* * *

Having finished her letter, Julia fanned it to make sure the ink was dry, then folded it, sealed it, and wrote "Mr. John Pickett" on the outside. Once she was certain this, too, was dry, she turned to the window, pushed open the sash, and dropped the letter into the void, leaning over the sill to watch as it fluttered to the ground. She closed the window, wincing at the screech of poorly fitted wood against wood. Almost immediately, there came a knock at her door; clearly, the sound had attracted the notice of Flynn, her supposed lover. She quickly gathered up her writing supplies, then cast a quick glance about the small room in search of anything else that might betray her. Finding nothing that might arouse suspicion, she stuffed the writing materials underneath the bed, then crossed to the door and opened it.

"Yes?" she prompted, unsurprised to discover Flynn standing in the corridor just outside her door. "What is it?"

"Just makin' sure you're not after doin' anything reckless," he said, his gaze shifting from her face to some point over her shoulder—the window, she had no doubt.

"No. I merely opened the window, thinking fresh air might be welcome, but the wind is a bit too keen, so I was obliged to close it again."

"Aye, and there's no tree you might be climbin' down now, is there?" he asked in mock sympathy. "If that's all, then I'll be biddin' you a good night. Best get some sleep, Mrs. P. We've a long way to go in the mornin'."

And that, she supposed, was that. Clearly, he suspected her of nothing more than looking for an opportunity to escape. And so she was, but she would bide her time until she could be sure such an attempt would have a reasonable opportunity of success. Until then, there was nothing she could do but try, as he said, to get some sleep. She removed her shoes, stockings, and dress—the latter sadly crushed from being worn for at least three days on end—then snuffed the candle and lay down in her undergarments.

She ought to feel rather pleased with herself; she had contrived to carry out one small act of rebellion beneath Flynn's very nose. More importantly, she had seen to John's safety. At best, he would decipher her message and act accordingly; at worst (and she considered this unlikely), he would take her letter at face value and, believing himself to be abandoned, return to London without making any further effort to reclaim his errant wife. Either way, her purpose would be accomplished. Yes, she should be pleased.

And yet, the only thing she felt was loneliness. Even in the days following her first husband's murder, even before love had blossomed between her and the surprisingly youthful Bow Street Runner charged with discovering Lord Field-hurst's killer, she had known that she could rely upon him, that she had only to send for him and he would be there. Now there was no one and nothing to rely upon except her own wits, and she was not at all certain that they were up to the challenge. She had never felt so completely alone in her life.

No sooner had the thought formed in her brain than she felt a slight fluttering sensation in her abdomen, almost as if she had swallowed a butterfly. She had not felt the baby move before, but she recognized it at once, and realized that a part of him was with her still, and would remain with her whatever the next day brought, or the next. She cupped her hand over the slight swell of her abdomen and closed her eyes.

She was not alone anymore.

* * *

Pickett and his Irregulars arose the following morning and walked the short distance to the harbor. Three of the four had fortified themselves with a substantial breakfast before undertaking what promised to be a long day at sea—even an easy crossing could not be accomplished in less than seventeen hours—but on this occasion Pickett steadfastly refused his brother-in-law's urging. In spite of a childhood spent mudlarking along the banks of the Thames and a youth spent unloading coal from the lighters that arrived in London almost daily from Newcastle, Pickett had gone to sea only once before in his life—a jaunt that had ended with his head hanging over the gunwale. In fact, his only agreeable memory of the experience had come in its immediate aftermath, when Julia (rather, Lady Fieldhurst, as she had been at the time) had discovered his sorry state and insisted upon tucking him into her own bed to recover. Although she had been regrettably absent from it at the time, the recollection was nonetheless pleasant enough that, after he and his present companions had purchased tickets, boarded the boat, and located their two tiny cabins, Pickett stretched out on the narrow cot, closed his eyes, and tried to imagine that she might enter at any minute and lay a gentle hand upon his forehead.

The wind off St. George's Channel was keen, but neither Carson nor Thomas had been at sea before, and both were determined to remain on deck regardless of any discomforts, so as not to miss a moment of the experience. As for Jamie, he was well-acquainted with the troop ships that had conveyed him and his fellow soldiers from their native shores to fight Boney on the Continent, so it was not the novelty of the experience that kept him out of his cabin, but the knowledge that his young brother-in-law would prefer to suffer in privacy. And so Pickett was left alone below deck, drifting in and out of wakefulness and alternating between impatience to reach the coast of Ireland and dread of what might be awaiting him there. But it was better not to think of that. Better, surely, to lie here and concentrate on the rise and fall of the hull beneath him; there were those, he recollected, rolling over with a groan, who found the movement soothing. Then again, there were those who enjoyed riding on horseback. Pickett couldn't understand them, either.

"John?" Pickett was roused from an uneasy sleep by a hushed voice and a hand shaking him by the shoulder. "Sorry to wake you, old fellow, but we'll be docking soon."

Pickett opened his eyes, and found the cabin in semidarkness. Beyond the porthole, seagulls shrieked and men shouted orders, and suddenly their craft gave a jerk as the ropes mooring it to the dock were pulled taut.

"We'll be allowed to disembark soon," Jamie continued. "I thought you might want a few minutes to collect yourself first."

"Oh—yes—thank you."

"Mr. Pickett, sir?" Thomas appeared in the low doorway. "Shall I collect your bag now?"

"Yes, thank you," Pickett said again.

As Jamie dragged his own valise from beneath the cot, Pickett heaved himself to his feet with an effort, and the three men climbed the short ladder to join Carson on deck. The wind had whipped a ruddy flush into Harry's cheeks, and his golden hair was attractively windblown. *It would be*, thought Pickett, disgusted.

Looking about him, he saw that they were not moored in a harbor adjoining the sea, as they had been in Holyhead, but had sailed up the River Liffey right into Dublin. Although a few ships strained at their ropes as if impatient to put to sea, there appeared to be little activity, and the cranes that had been erected along both banks for loading and unloading cargo now stood idle. Some distance upriver, the north bank was dominated by a large building whose stately columns and domed roof appeared the equal of anything to be seen in London.

"So, what do we do now, chief?" Carson asked.

"We find Mountjoy Square," Pickett said.

Jamie withdrew the watch from his pocket and checked the time. "I hate to countermand orders, but we'd do better to find lodging for the night, and start fresh in the morning." No doubt anticipating Pickett's objections, he added, "Remember that during the summertime, the farther north you go, the later the sun sets. It's almost ten o'clock. The way I see it, we're going to have to go door-to-door asking after this man, and I doubt you'll endear yourself to any of the residents by knocking them up at such an hour."

Reluctantly, Pickett was forced to admit that he was probably right. And so, after making their way down the gangway, they located the most respectable-looking of the inns that clung to the banks of the river, and went inside. Once again, Pickett requested two rooms, and upon signing his name, the woman behind the counter was moved to exclamation.

"Don't be tellin' me *you're* this Mr. John Pickett! Well, I must say I've been after expectin'—but never mind that! I have somethin' for you."

She reached beneath the counter, and Pickett braced himself for the worst. What would it be this time—another finger, or would his tormentor try something different this time? A toe, perhaps, or an ear? But no, she held out a folded and sealed paper of the cheaper sort. Pickett caught a glimpse of his own name written in a familiar hand, and it required all his self-control not to snatch it from the woman's fingers.

"When was this left here?" he asked, trying to sound nonchalant when he could hardly hear his own voice for the sound of his heart hammering against his ribs.

"Two days ago, it was—or was it three? Aye, I believe it was three."

Pickett took his prize to the window, where the last of the day's sunlight reflecting off the water provided enough light by which to read. Three days ago. As of three days ago, she had been alive, and had stood in this very room, leaving a letter for him. He took a deep breath, then broke the seal and spread open the paper. He reached the end, and looked up to find three faces regarding him expectantly.

"It's her." He handed the letter to the nearest of his compatriots, which happened to be Carson. "She's alive, or at least she was, three days ago."

"Do you mean to tell me," Harry demanded upon reaching the end and surrendering the unsatisfying correspondence to Jamie, "that this isn't an abduction at all, but an elopement? That we're chasing all over the country after a woman who doesn't want to be found?"

"Of course not," Pickett said contemptuously, then turned away to ask the proprietress for a candle, as well as paper, ink, and quill.

"I must say, he seems to be taking it awfully well," Carson observed to the other two men. "Unless, of course, he's lost his wits entirely."

"He's onto something, you watch and see," Thomas predicted confidently, looking up from the letter he had just received from Jamie. "Mrs. Pickett wouldn't leave him by choice, no matter what she might be forced to put down on paper." He was in a better position to know than any of them, having on more than one occasion entered a room unexpectedly to discover master and mistress locked in a passionate embrace.

"You think someone forced her to write this—"

Carson's question was interrupted by the return of Pickett, bearing a tallow candle set in a pewter holder, and cupping one hand protectively about the flame. He set it down on a small table beneath the window and turned to his valet.

"Give me the letter, Thomas."

Thomas was quick to obey, and Pickett took the letter from him and held it a few inches above the flame.

Carson turned to address Thomas *sotto voce*. "If she hasn't run off and left him, why is he burning her letter?"

No one bothered to answer him, for their attention was all for the paper in Pickett's hand. It was not burning, but as the paper grew warm from the flame beneath it, dark lines slowly began to appear, underscoring certain letters or words.

My dearest John, it now read, *I sit here with my teacup at my elbow—sugar, milk, and especially lemon, just the way I like it—contemplating our past, and my own future. Much as I love you (and always will), I cannot persist in a marriage that has brought me equal parts despair and bliss. Marriage is meant to last "till death do us part," I know, but surely you will agree with my own view, that it would be better to not waste precious time in trying to fix ours, which is long past being mended. And so I must beg you not to waste your energies in pursuit, but to give me up. To do otherwise can only bring pain to us both. Please know that although I must bid you farewell, there remains a part of my heart that will always be yours.*

Pickett dipped the quill into the ink pot and began to copy the underlined letters along the bottom margin of the paper.

HETHERINGTONESCAPEDANDMEANSTOKILLYOUDONOTC OMEFORME

Having recently deciphered a far more complex message written in the same code, Pickett found that this time dividing the letters into words was the work of a moment:

HETHERINGTON ESCAPED AND MEANS TO KILL YOU DO NOT COME FOR ME

"Well, I'll be damned!" exclaimed Carson, leaning in for a closer look.

"Probably," agreed Pickett.

"But—how did you know?"

"I broke just such a code last month, in the Lake District." Of course, that had been the merest stroke of good fortune, as he'd been seated, and had held the letter up where Julia could read it over his shoulder; the candle had done the rest. Still, he wasn't about to admit that to Harry Carson.

"Yes, I heard all about that," Carson said impatiently. "But how did you even know to look for such a thing?"

Pickett laid the quill aside and looked up at him. "Julia doesn't take lemon in her tea." While Carson pondered this revelation, he added, "You know, there are advantages to staying with one woman long enough to learn something about her."

14

In Which Julia Becomes
the Houseguest of a Madman

The carriage turned off the main road, and a knot formed in the pit of Julia's stomach; it appeared they were about to reach their destination at last. The trees lining the long drive were badly in need of pruning, their limbs meeting together overhead to form a green tunnel that cast the interior of the carriage into gloom. Beneath them, long grasses had pushed their way up through what had once been raked gravel, and now made a swishing sound as they bowed beneath the carriage that passed over them, bending their feathery heads and scattering their seeds.

At last the darkness lifted as the avenue of trees opened out to reveal what must have once been a very fine house of gray stone. "Fine" was not the word she would use to describe it now. Several of its windows were broken out, and whole sections of the roof were devoid of shingles. The parkland, although lush, had been so long neglected that the hedges fronting the house almost covered the ground-floor windows. Julia was certain she had never visited the estate—in fact, she had never been to Ireland at all—and yet it seemed strangely familiar.

And then she remembered. She had never been here, but she had once seen a painting of this same house in more prosperous days, hanging in the bedchamber of a woman who had grown up within these very walls. For this was the childhood home of Mrs. Brigid Hetherington, Irish-born wife of Robert Hetherington, convicted traitor and escaped felon. Half a century before her husband plotted the unsuccessful overthrow of Carlisle Castle, the young Brigid's father had committed a similar crime, throwing in his lot with that of a French pirate who had succeeded in seizing, at least for a time, the castle at Carrickfergus. The property of traitors, Julia knew, was forfeit to the Crown—which had apparently allowed it to fall to rack and ruin. She wondered if a similar fate awaited Robert Hetherington's own property in the Lake District. It appeared that he, not daring to return to that estate so soon after his escape from prison, had taken up residence instead in the abandoned house of his long-deceased father-in-law.

In any case, it seemed her questions were about to be answered. The driver—Bohannan, Flynn had called him—drew the carriage to a stop before the great double doors, and a moment later the door of the carriage was flung open.

"Here we are," Bohannan announced unnecessarily, before falling back to allow them room to descend.

Flynn slid off the seat, ducked his head, and leaped down

from the carriage, then lowered the step. "Mrs. Pickett," he said, holding out his hand to assist her in disembarking.

"I'll remain here, thank you," she said with a confidence she was far from feeling.

His face turned dark with anger. "You'll come inside if I have to be throwin' you over my shoulder like a sack of meal and carryin' you myself!"

If his expression was anything to judge by, she didn't doubt he would make good on the threat. She glanced past him at the foreboding structure and resolved that, whatever awaited her within those crumbling walls, she would meet it with as much dignity as she could muster; after all, dignity was very nearly all she had left to her at this point. Without protest, she took his outstretched hand and descended from the carriage with all the grace and elegance drilled into her by her longsuffering governess.

"A very wise decision, Mrs. Pickett," Flynn said, drawing her hand through his arm.

She had not intended to accept his escort beyond the point when her foot first touched the ground. She was surprised, and a little dismayed, to discover that his arm trembled beneath her fingers; clearly, her captor was as nervous as she was. The thought was not a reassuring one. If he, who worked hand in glove with Mr. Hetherington, was afraid of the man, then what hope did she have?

She very much feared she was about to find out. Bohannan had preceded them up the stairs onto the portico, and flung open the door as they approached. At least, she suspected that was his intention. But the hinges were rusty from disuse, and their driver was obliged to grip the ornate handle with both hands and pull with all his might before the heavy wooden panel yawned open, groaning in protest at the invasion.

The three stepped inside, and in spite of the neglected hedges that prevented the sunlight from entering, Julia could see that they were standing in a hall with a marble-tiled floor of alternating black and white squares, like an oversized chessboard. *Check, or checkmate?* she wondered, blinking as her eyes adjusted to the gloom.

"I expect Himself will be waitin' upstairs," Bohannan speculated, and Julia could not help noticing that, although Flynn agreed that this was very likely, neither man appeared to be particularly eager to climb the curving staircase in search of him.

If there was one thing marriage to the late Lord Fieldhurst had taught her, it was how to present a brave face to the world even when her own world was crumbling around her. It was to this long-ago lesson that she now sought recourse. "By 'Himself,' I assume you mean Mr. Hetherington," she said briskly, taking a perverse sort of pleasure in betraying less fear than either of her abductors. But then, she supposed she had less to lose than they. Whatever she said or did, the end result for her would very likely be the same; they, on the other hand, had to deal with humoring the whims of a madman. "If he is expecting us, I suggest we not keep him waiting."

She strode across the hall to the foot of the steps and placed one hand on the banister. "Ugh!" With her best imitation of her mother's manner, she released the railing and regarded her dirty hand with distaste. "Needs dusting," she pronounced, then picked up her skirts and climbed the stairs.

"Flynn?" a voice bellowed as she reached the floor above. "Bohannan? Is that you?"

"No," she called. "It's Mrs. Pickett. I daresay your lackeys will be along directly."

She had followed the sound of the familiar voice down the hall as she spoke, and now stood in the doorway of the room whence that voice had come. Here her carefully feigned confidence suffered a check. The man sitting in a faded wing chair before the fire was the same man with whom she had dined in the Lake District, but he appeared to have aged ten years in the few weeks since she had last seen him. His hair was whiter than she remembered, and unkempt wisps flew out from his head at all angles. His face seemed to sag, as if it had been fashioned from wax and left too close to the fire.

"Mr. Hetherington," she said, being careful not to allow any hint of repugnance to show in her voice. "It's a pleasure to see you again."

It was a lie, of course; she would have been quite happy to go the rest of her life without seeing him again. In fact, she would have very much preferred it, for her husband's sake as well as her own. But here he was, and here she was—albeit against her will—so there was nothing for it but to try to placate the man for as long as possible.

"It's a pleasure to see you as well, my dear," he said, beckoning for her to enter. "Although, as charming as your company is, I must admit that my enjoyment of it pales in comparison to the eagerness with which I await your husband's arrival."

"Does it indeed?" Julia seated herself on the sofa he indicated, trying not to sneeze as a cloud of dust arose from its cushions. "Then it pains me to have to tell you that he will not be joining us."

" 'Not' you say?" He regarded her in some distress, and for a moment she wondered if she was making a tactical error in provoking him.

"I'm afraid not. He is on an investigation, you see." She paused for effect, then added, "In Dunbury."

"Ah!" His brow cleared at once. "Then he is chasing after mares' nests. It was I who sent him to Dunbury, you see."

Yes, definitely a chess match, she thought, recalling the squares of black and white marble on the hall floor below. But it was her move now, and so she made it. "That is what Mr. Flynn said, although I confess I fail to understand why, if you wanted him here, you would send him on a fool's errand fully three hundred miles in the opposite direction."

"I needed you unprotected," he explained. He glanced past her in the direction of the door through which she had entered, and she knew without looking that Flynn and Bohannan had joined them. "My lackeys, as you call them, have been all that is obliging, but I fear even their best efforts would be no match for a determined bridegroom—and one, moreover, with all the authority of Bow Street at his back. But speaking of Mssrs. Flynn and Bohannan, I trust they treated you well? I shall be very displeased if they did not." This last was said in a more threatening tone, and directed toward some point over her shoulder.

The suggestion that one might be abducted in a manner one found acceptable was outrageous enough to provoke Julia into responding more tartly than was perhaps wise. "If I overlook the fact that they coshed me over the head and removed me forcibly from my home—a feat which is quite beyond my capabilities at the moment—then I can have no cause for complaint."

"Did they indeed?" Robert Hetherington scowled fiercely at the men behind her. "Which one committed this atrocious act?"

"It was Mr. Flynn," she said, feeling oddly like a talebearer for doing so. "And yet, I suspect his treatment of me pales next to your own plans."

"Well, yes," confessed Hetherington, unrepentant. "But my orders were that they were to do nothing to you that might cause young Mr. Pickett to turn from you in revulsion—no 'fate worse than death,' if I may be permitted to speak so crudely. Nor must your husband be allowed the consolation of believing you to have been released from any earthly suffering. No, he is to endure all the agonies of seeing a beloved wife slain before his eyes."

He spoke as if this were the most reasonable course of action in the world, and she found his rational demeanor more terrifying than any amount of insane ranting would have been.

"Why do you hate him so?" Her own voice was little more than a whisper.

"Why?" He seemed genuinely surprised by the question. "Because he did no less to me."

"Mr. Hetherington, I am truly sorry for the loss of your wife. I liked her very much, and wish I might have known her better. But surely you know her death was an accident."

"If that is so—a supposition which I beg leave to doubt—then it was an accident for which he was responsible."

She realized nothing she might say would budge him from this stance, so she tried another approach. "But is it fair to make an innocent person suffer for actions in which he or she played no part?"

"No, of course not." Hetherington readily conceded the point. "And yet my wife, only a child at the time, endured unspeakable cruelty in retaliation for the actions of her father. A woman may choose her husband, but no child can choose its father. You chose your husband, Mrs. Pickett, so your fate is linked with his."

She was mistaken; this was no chess match, but a game of whist—and her only chance at taking the trick lay in playing her trump card. She took a deep, steadying breath and placed it, figuratively speaking, on the table. "I did indeed choose Mr. Pickett, and I would do so again. I don't know if your wife told you or not, but Mr. Pickett and I are expecting our first child in December." She gave him a moment to ponder the significance of this statement, then added gently, "As you said yourself, no child may choose its father."

For a long moment, he stared at her in stunned silence. Then his ravaged face split in a wide grin. "Why, no, Brigid didn't tell me. But this—this is *wonderful!*"

"Yes, it is wonderful," Julia said with all the sincerity at her command. In fact, she had never dreamed it would be so easy. "Thank you, sir. I knew you could not—"

"Now he will be left to mourn not only his wife, but his child as well!"

The delight in his voice at the prospect caused the blood to run cold in her veins. "But—"

"Four times"—he tucked his thumb down and waved the remaining four fingers in her face—"four times my Brigid miscarried a child, thanks to internal injuries she suffered at the hands of Englishmen like your husband! I only regret that I can kill but one of his!"

"Mr. Hetherington, no woman should have to experience what your wife endured, but my husband was not even born at the time! Surely you must see that!"

Even as she said the words, she knew they were futile; he was beyond reason, beyond rational thought. Unexpectedly, help came from the last place she would have looked for it.

"Here now, I'll not be a party to this." Julia turned and identified the speaker as Bohannan, the carriage driver whom she had heard speak only once during the long journey from London. "I know you promised to help us, Mr. H., and don't be thinkin' I'm not grateful for it. But it seems to me that if Ireland has to resort to murderin' pregnant women in order to win our freedom, then maybe we're not deservin' to be free."

Julia held her breath as Hetherington's attention shifted from her to the man at her back. "You were singing a different tune when you approached me in Carlisle Prison," he said. "Still, I wouldn't want to force you into anything you find morally objectionable. If you wish to leave, you may do so at any time."

"Don't be thinkin' I won't," Bohannan replied, then turned and started for the door.

He had scarcely taken two steps when Hetherington pulled out a pistol and shot him squarely in the back. Julia could only stare in horror, first at the man seated next to her with the gun, still smoking, in his hand, then at the pile of skin and blood and bone that only moments before had been a living human being.

One thing was certain. Robert Hetherington had lost whatever grip on sanity he had once retained, and although she might understand the reason for his descent into madness, she could not afford to make the mistake of pitying him.

Not if she hoped to survive.

15

Which Finds John Pickett
Making Inquiries in Dublin

P ickett stood at the corner of Mountjoy Square with his companions, surveying the incomplete quadrangle on which construction had begun almost twenty years earlier. Eventually, he supposed, the square would be fully enclosed by the handsome brick residences sprouting up along its perimeter, each with four stories and a broad fan-shaped window over its door; for now, at least, its unfinished state would mean fewer places in which to search for Mr. James Sullivan.

"Let's each take a side," he said. "I'll take the south." It had been the first one begun, and so was the nearest to completion.

The north and west sides went to Carson and Jamie, respectively; his brother-in-law had no experience in investigation, but Jamie was nobody's fool, and Pickett trusted him to know what to do without lengthy explanations.

That left Thomas to make inquiries along the eastern side of the square, where only a few houses had as yet been built.

"Me?" his valet asked, brightening at being given an active part of the investigation. "I'm to have a street all to myself?"

"It'll save time that way," Pickett explained. "Four streets; four men. The houses are still under construction, and some of them may be vacant. If anyone answers the door, ask them if they know where you might find a Mr. James Sullivan. Don't let on that he might be implicated in any crime. In fact, don't even hint that anything untoward is going on."

"I spent four years in service to his late lordship," Thomas replied with some dignity. "He used to have me deliver messages to the Foreign Office. I know how to be discreet, sir."

Pickett clapped him on the shoulder. "Good man!"

"Look here," Carson protested, "wouldn't it be better to tell them at once what's in the wind? It seems to me that time is of the essence, and who knows what might be—"

"You don't have to remind me of that, Harry," Pickett interrupted. "Believe me, I'm well aware of it. But we're going to be asking about their neighbor, perhaps even their friend. At best, they might clamp their lips shut and refuse to talk to us at all; at worst, they could deliberately put us off the scent with false information."

"Yes, but with a potential reward for giving evidence—"

Pickett sighed. He supposed he might have made the same assumption at one time, during his years on the Foot Patrol, but not any longer. "Look about you," he told Carson, making a sweeping motion with his arm that took in the broad square and the stately residences dotting its perimeter. "Does it look as if any of these people are likely to be in need of funds?"

"I suppose you're right," said Carson, reluctantly conceding the point.

"What do I say if he lives there, or if they tell me which house is his?" Thomas asked, all eagerness to play at being a Bow Street runner, at least for a little while.

"In that case, beg to be excused while you fetch your companions," Pickett told him. "We'll meet at the sundial, shall we?" He gestured toward a granite structure in the center of the square.

The four men agreed, then broke up to pursue their individual assignments. Pickett strode across the square to the first house on the end of the block, then stepped up onto the portico and knocked. It was opened a moment later by a butler as starchy as any who might be found in Mayfair.

"Sullivan residence?" Pickett asked. "Mr. James Sullivan?"

He had not really expected to be so fortunate on his first attempt, and so was not disappointed when the butler informed him that no one of that name resided there.

"I understand. Can you tell me in which of these houses"—he raised one arm in a sweeping gesture that encompassed the entire square—"I might find him?"

"No, sir, I fear I cannot. If you would care to wait, however, I might inquire of Mr. Walsh."

"Thank you," Pickett said, sincerely grateful for a

courtesy he had not anticipated. "I would be obliged to you."

The butler allowed him to enter—another consideration he had not expected—and Pickett waited in the foyer while the man went in search of his master. He returned a minute later, bearing disappointing news.

"Mr. Walsh sends his regrets, but says he can think of no such person, and certainly no resident of this square by that name. However, there is a Mr. James Donovan in Mountjoy West, if perhaps you might be mistaken in the name?"

Pickett shook his head. "No, I'm afraid there can be no mistake. I thank you for taking the trouble though, and please convey my thanks to Mr. Walsh."

Alas, it was only the first of many such disappointments. By the time he reached the end of Mountjoy Square South— nineteen houses in all—he had not found one person who had ever heard of Mr. James Sullivan, much less who knew which house might be his. In fact, a nagging suspicion was beginning to form in Pickett's brain—a suspicion which appeared to be confirmed when the little group met at the sundial on the green.

"No luck, sir," Thomas reported. As there were fewer houses on his street, he had been the first to finish his assigned task, and had been awaiting the other three with mingled hope that they might have better luck, and disappointment that he was not to be the one to divulge the desired information. "Not only does Mr. Sullivan not live in any of the houses on the east side, but no one seems to have even heard of him."

"Same here," put in Carson, while Jamie nodded.

Pickett sighed in resignation. "An assumed name, then. I

feared as much."

Was Julia held captive somewhere behind one of these elegant brick façades, or had she been taken somewhere else entirely? And if so, where? As matters stood now, he had no idea where to go or what to do next. He recalled again the letter he had removed from the pocket of a dying man, the folded and sealed paper bearing the name and direction of the man for whom they now sought—a man who, it now seemed, did not exist, and had very likely never existed at all. If he could only remember the house number, he would pound on the door and demand answers of whoever opened it, regardless of the name they gave. But in the absence of even this rough-and-ready plan of action, then what? Once again, the feeling of utter helplessness assailed him.

"If anyone has any ideas," he addressed his three companions, "I would love to hear them."

The silence that followed this invitation told its own tale.

At last, Carson spoke. "I keep thinking about that finger."

Pickett closed his eyes as if to block out the image. "I'm trying not to."

"No, but listen. If somebody dug up a dead body and mutilated it, wouldn't you think someone would know about it? I mean, even if they contrived to bury the body again by morning, anyone could have seen that the dirt had been disturbed."

"Very likely," Pickett agreed with exaggerated patience. "But the thing was quite possibly, even probably, done somewhere other than Wales."

"Yes, but don't you see?" Carson insisted. "If someone

was going about desecrating graves—even only the one grave—wouldn't it be important enough to be talked about—mentioned in a newspaper, say?"

Pickett opened his eyes and regarded his colleague with dawning respect. "Harry, I think you just might be on to something."

"You don't have to sound so surprised," retorted Carson, stung. "You're not the only one who knows anything about investigating, you know."

* * *

Citizens of Dublin who wished to stay abreast of events in the wider world had several publications—more than thirty, in fact—to which they might turn for information. John Pickett, who had more reason than most to desire enlightenment as to recent events, was resolved to examine them all, if that was what it took to find what he sought. The *Freeman's Journal*, as its name implied, took a particular interest in the cause of Irish independence; if a single instance of grave-robbing should happen to be connected, however loosely, to the promotion of that objective, it was likely that the event would be given very little attention, perhaps even be ignored altogether rather than run the risk of casting the proponents of the cause in a negative light. On the other hand, the *Dublin Gazette* was the local iteration of the English *London Gazette*, and would certainly reflect the views of its English counterpart. One smaller, weekly publication was devoted to the interests of Catholics, and another to Protestants; either of these might be sufficiently offended by the desecration of a grave and the dismemberment of a corpse that they would report such a violation, no matter where it might have occurred or who might be responsible. Finally, a number of broadsheets addressed the particular concerns of commerce, manufacturing, or agriculture. These, Pickett decided, could be ignored unless and until all other avenues had been explored in vain.

Having narrowed the field to the four most promising possibilities, Pickett assigned a man to cover each. He himself would take the *Dublin Gazette* while Carson took the *Freeman's Journal* and Jamie examined the Protestant periodical. This left its Catholic counterpart—the smallest and therefore the easiest of the four to examine from first page to last—for Thomas's perusal.

"How far do I need to go back, sir?" asked that young man, determined to devote himself thoroughly to the task.

"Not far," Pickett assured him, unaware that this was exactly what his valet least wished to hear. "It's published weekly, not daily, so the last two issues—three, at the very most—should be sufficient. Just be sure you take the time to read them thoroughly."

"The—the whole thing, sir?" Thomas protested feebly, struggling to reconcile the tales of danger and bravado recounted by Mr. Carson with the prospect of spending hours bent over the printed page. "Surely the headlines—"

"The whole thing," Pickett echoed firmly. "It might not be mentioned in the headlines. It might be given no more than a mention—buried in a longer article on, say, atrocities committed by Protestants against Catholics, or defending Catholics against similar charges against them made by

Protestants, or an article on general lawlessness."

"Yes, sir," Thomas said with a marked lack of enthusiasm.

"I know it sounds tedious," Pickett said, not without sympathy. "It *is* tedious. It's like I told you before: nine parts of any investigation is tedium, no matter what Carson may say to the contrary. And at the moment, this lead is our best hope for discovering where Ju—Mrs. Pickett may have been taken, so I'm going to follow it until it leads me to her. Or until it runs out, or until it points me in another direction. Whichever comes first."

"Yes, sir," Thomas said again, more energetically this time.

The four men split up, and after making inquiries as to the location of the newspaper's offices, Pickett set out for the Custom House Printing Office in Crane Lane, a narrow thoroughfare just off Dame Street, and asked if he might have a look at the archives.

"Is there anything in particular you're lookin' for?" asked the clerk who ushered him down the stairs and into a dark, cavernous basement room where back issues of the newspaper were stored.

"I was wondering if you—the publisher, that is—has run a story lately about any graves being disturbed."

"By the resurrection men, you mean?"

"Not exactly," Pickett said. "I don't think the grave robbers were interested in supplying the medical profession with cadavers so much as they were in obtaining one body— the body of a woman—for their own purposes."

"Begorra!" breathed the clerk, wide-eyed.

"Nothing like that," Pickett put in quickly, realizing the man was entertaining visions of lurid orgiastic rites, no doubt performed around a bonfire beneath a full moon. "Something more in the nature of a—a prank."

"Some prank!"

"Exactly. Do you recall the newspaper printing an article about such a thing?"

The clerk shook his head. "No, sir, I'm afraid not. And if you don't mind my sayin' so, it doesn't seem the sort of thing I'd be likely to forget!"

"I don't doubt it. But if you have no objection, I should like to look through the newspapers myself, just to be sure."

To his profound relief, the clerk showed no sign of taking offense at this apparent lack of confidence in his memory, merely lighting a lamp positioned on a work table and giving Pickett a brief overview of which of the boxes and crates stacked haphazardly against the walls corresponded with what dates. Pickett thanked him in a manner that, he hoped, also served as a dismissal; he had no desire to conduct his search while at the same time fielding questions from a man clearly agog for further details about the act of vandalism that had brought Pickett to his door.

The *Dublin Gazette* had been in print for more than a century, and its archive was correspondingly massive. Pickett, regarding the stacks of crates and boxes, was thankful he didn't have to look beyond the last couple of weeks; even that abbreviated search was likely to take all day, and very possibly more. And in the meantime, Julia was—where?

Enduring what? The clerk's false assumptions had been almost amusing, in their way, but they had resurrected fears Pickett had been trying, with mixed success, to hold at bay from the moment he'd learned she had been taken.

Still, he'd insisted that Thomas examine each issue thoroughly, regardless of the time such an examination required, and he refused to demand less of himself than he required of his valet. Heaving a sigh, he moved the crate containing the most recent issues to the table, drew up a stool, and began to read.

It soon transpired that the *Dublin Gazette* was little more than a mouthpiece for its English counterpart. Its motto was "Published by Authority," and it became clear that "authority," in this case, meant the English government. Many, perhaps even most, of its articles had appeared a few days earlier in the *London Gazette*, and the few that were original seemed designed to subtly—or not so subtly— emphasize the subordinate status of its Irish readers. Reaching for yet another issue, Pickett doubted very much there would be any mention of desecrated graves at all, unless the event were offered as evidence of the inability of the Irish to govern themselves.

And then, just when he was ready to give up the *Dublin Gazette* as a lost cause, he discovered what he was looking for. It was not a long article; in fact, it was not an article at all, but a letter to the editor along the lines of "young people these days," in which the writer listed several complaints, beginning with garden-variety vandalism and progressing to shocking atrocities—including, as an example of the latter, the brief mention of an illegal exhumation conducted under cover of darkness and for no other purpose than the disfigurement of an unfortunate young woman's earthly remains. The letter was attributed to one Gerald Reilly, resident of a place called Summerhill in County Meath.

It wasn't much to go on—in fact, it might refer to another disfigurement of another young woman entirely—but at the moment, it was all he had. Pickett glanced about to make sure he was alone in the room, then withdrew a penknife from the pocket of his coat and carefully cut the letter out of the larger page. He folded the letter in half, then folded it again and tucked it into his pocket along with the knife. After returning the stack of newspapers to the crate and the crate to the proper shelf, he climbed the stairs, thanked the clerk for his assistance and assured him that, yes, he believed he had found what he'd sought.

Then he joined his three traveling companions at their appointed meeting place and informed them that they would be setting out at first light for County Meath.

16

*In Which Julia Gathers Information
and Bides Her Time*

Summerhill, when they reached it, proved to be a humble village whose only claims to distinction were the two stately homes in the vicinity: Summerhill House, the enormous Palladian edifice built for Lord Langford in the previous century, which crowned the summit of a hill overlooking the village; and, some few miles to the north, Dangan House, the childhood home of Sir Arthur Wellesley, recently appointed head of British forces in Portugal and, if Jamie were to be believed, a man for whom even greater achievements lay in store.

By contrast, the house Pickett sought was a modest abode, one of a string of attached dwellings lining the street across from the church. A patch of bare earth in the churchyard suggested a recent burial—or, perhaps, a reburial. *No wonder he took such an interest in a body being dug up*, Pickett thought as he strode up the short walk to the cottage door. *The exhumation took place practically on his doorstep.*

He was alone on this occasion, having pointed out to his companions, quite correctly, that the sight of no fewer than four Englishmen standing on his doorstep would not inspire any Irishman toward loquaciousness. And so, after inquiring at a public house where Mr. Gerald Reilly might be found, he had left Jamie, Carson, and Thomas refreshing themselves after the journey from the fruits of the pub's cellars while he paid a call on the author of the *Dublin Gazette*'s letter.

"Mr. Reilly?" he asked when the door was opened by an elderly man with thick white hair and blue eyes beneath bushy white eyebrows. In fact, he bore so marked a resemblance to Pickett's magistrate, Mr. Colquhoun, that Pickett resolved to ask upon his return to Bow Street whether his mentor had any relatives in Ireland. "Mr. Gerald Reilly?"

"Aye, that's m'name, don't wear it out."

It was not the most encouraging of welcomes, but having come this far, Pickett was not about to give up so easily.

"You wrote a letter," he said, fumbling in the inside pocket of his coat, "to the *Gazette.*"

He had, at least, the satisfaction of seeing the scowl lift from those eyebrows. "Aye, that I did, I'll not deny it. What of it?"

Having found the rectangle of paper he'd cut from the *Gazette*, Pickett offered it for the man's inspection. "You make mention of an 'illegal exhumation conducted under cover of darkness and for no other purpose than the disfigurement of an unfortunate young woman's earthly remains.' " By this time, Pickett had read and reread those lines so many times he could now recite them *verbatim*. He saw no reason to mention the fact that there was only one "m" in "exhumation."

Gerald Reilly's gaze shifted from Pickett to some point over his shoulder—the naked patch of dirt in the churchyard, he suspected.

"You've come about that, have you?" Reilly asked eagerly. "Mean to put a stop to it, I hope?"

"Er, not exactly," Pickett confessed, painfully aware that this admission might considerably hinder his cause. "I think I may know why it was done, if it's the body I think it may be."

"Just how many of them do you think there are?"

"Only the one, I hope. Can you tell me something about it—about her?"

Reilly noticed Pickett's self-correction, and nodded in approval. "Aye, you've got the right of it. She was once a living, breathing human being, and her body ought to be treated with respect, in honor of the person she used to be."

"And who was that?"

"My sister's girl. Died in childbirth, she did, and the babe with her." Again his gaze shifted to fix on something beyond Pickett's shoulder. "Didn't waste any time in getting her body back underground, mind you, but every time I step out my door or look out my front window, I see the bare dirt where poor Moira was dug up, and think of her. It was like losing her all over again, them digging her up like that."

"In your letter, you mention disfigurement," Pickett reminded him gently, trying to sound respectful and sympathetic while at the same time steering the conversation back to his own area of interest. "If you don't mind—if you have no objection to—"

Seeing his visitor floundering helplessly, Reilly took matters into his own hands. "What did they do to her, d'you mean? Well you may ask! Cut off one of her fingers, they did, the bastards!"

Pickett's heart began pounding to such an extent that he was surprised Mr. Reilly couldn't see his chest twitching. "Cut off one of her—"

"Aye, the little finger of her right hand. Mind, it would've been bad enough losing her to the resurrection men, but we could at least have taken some small comfort in knowing that a new medical discovery might have come of it. But this"—he made a vague gesture in the direction of the churchyard and the new grave—"why would a man do something like this?"

"A prank, perhaps—" Pickett began.

"A *prank?*" the Irishman echoed in disbelief. "D'you mean to tell me somebody thought this was *funny?*"

"A warning, then. Maybe even a threat." *Or a taunt*, he added mentally. *A way of saying "I've got your wife and there's not a bloody thing you can do about it."* Yes, Hetherington would certainly find that funny. But maybe, just maybe, it would be he who would have the last laugh. "Tell me, do you know of any estate hereabouts that—I'm afraid I don't know the name, but it would have been confiscated by the Crown about fifty years ago, after the battle of Carrickfergus. The owner—"

"Oh, you're thinking of the old Lynch place. Fairacres,

its name was, although it's not looking so fair these days, or so they say."

"Can you tell me how to get there?"

Something of Pickett's eagerness must have shown in his face, for Reilly frowned. "Aye, but you won't find anyone there. It's stood empty for almost fifty years."

"I understand." Pickett nodded in agreement, although he suspected it wasn't nearly as empty as Reilly supposed. "I just—there are—reasons—I need to find the place."

The older man obliged by giving the necessary directions, all the while regarding Pickett warily, as if he suspected the poor fellow of having lost his wits. As well he might, the Irishman decided, if someone had been sending him dismembered fingers as some sort of joke.

Pickett thanked Reilly for his help, adding his belated condolences for the man's loss—although it was difficult to sound properly sober and sympathetic when everything in him wanted to sing and shout and laugh and dance and, finally, break down and sob from sheer relief.

Julia was less than five miles away.

And he was going to reclaim her.

* * *

Has it been three days or four? Julia wondered as she stole a glance around the table at her dinner companions. The time they'd spent on the journey had been marked by differences in the various posting-houses where they had broken their journey at the end of every day, and Julia had done her best to keep count of these in order to form some idea of where they were taking her. But since they had reached their destination—which she knew must be somewhere in Ireland—the days had begun to run together in a blur, like a watercolor left out in the rain.

She could not complain of the treatment she had received; she was afforded all the consideration that one might give an honored guest. And yet it was very clear that she was not to be allowed to leave the house. When on the very first day she had attempted an exploratory walk about the grounds for the purpose of determining a likely escape route— although she had offered, as a belated excuse, a desire to exercise her limbs after being shut up for so long in the carriage—Flynn had discovered her and escorted her back to the house, and at dinner that night her host had given her a gentle scold.

"For you might have fallen, perhaps even twisted your ankle, and no one knowing where you were or what had happened to you," he'd pointed out, as if he were a doting uncle and she a small and not particularly intelligent child. "If you want to go out, you have only to ask, and either Flynn here or I myself will escort you."

She'd found his solicitous manner nothing short of terrifying. The genial host and the man who hadn't hesitated to shoot Bohannan in the back might have been two completely different people.

While she could not bring herself to request Mr. Hetherington's escort, she had on more than one occasion been so desperate to escape her prison that she'd asked Flynn to accompany her on a walk about the neglected grounds. One of these walks had taken them near the stable, and Flynn had been displeased to discover one of the wide double doors standing slightly ajar, swinging gently on its hinges in the breeze.

"Stay right there," Flynn instructed her. "I'll be watchin' you, in case you'll be getting' any ideas." With this warning, he strode away toward the stables.

Until that moment, Julia had not thought of the horses that had pulled the carriage. Were they trained to the saddle as well? Even if she were able to escape the house unseen, she had no habit or crop, and would no doubt be obliged to saddle her own hack, but these circumstances, though far from ideal, should not present any insurmountable obstacle; Papa had been determined that his daughters should be able to ride under any circumstances, even going so far as to put his little girls into the saddle astride and in their pantalets, deaf to Mama's shocked and horrified protests. No, no daughter of Sir Thaddeus Runyon would balk at making her escape bareback and wearing the narrowest skirts she owned, if that were her only option.

But now, as Julia tried frantically to see what she could of the stable through the open door, she was disappointed to catch no glimpse of either horses or carriage. In fact, the stable—or at least that part of it that she could see—appeared to be empty except for a number of crates, barrels, and sacks, all piled haphazardly just inside the doors. And then she could see no more, for Flynn pushed first one door closed and then the other, shutting off her view before turning and making his way back to her.

She would have loved to ask about the contents of the

stores, but dared not betray any interest. And even if she did, he would probably fob her off by claiming they contained oats for the horses—an answer that might have made sense had it been September instead of July, when the fields contained sufficient grazing as to make such large quantities of fodder unnecessary—indeed, even undesirable, since any resident rats would have made inroads into the supply long before the horses had much need for it.

And so she said nothing, but kept her eyes and ears open for any details that might give her escape, when she made it, a greater chance at success. In the meantime, an unexpected benefit of her supposed resignation to her captive state soon presented itself. For since she displayed no intention of attempting an escape, her dinner companions grew less careful in their speech than they had been on that first night.

"I thought I'd be goin' to the village in the mornin'," Flynn told Hetherington. He sounded uncertain, as if tacitly asking for approval, and it occurred to Julia that he, in his own way, was just as frightened of the man as she was. "See about hirin' a wagon and team to be deliverin' the package."

Hetherington reached into the inside pocket of his coat and withdrew a roll of bills, which he tossed across the table to Flynn. "That should do it, I think."

"Shall I be askin' for a few lads to come back with me and help load it?" Flynn asked, pocketing the money.

Hetherington appeared to consider the matter, but shook his head. "I think not. No need to take unnecessary risks, not when we're so close."

"I don't suppose—?" The rest of the question was left

unsaid, but Flynn's gaze shifted rather pointedly to her and then back to Hetherington.

"Let me remind you that Mrs. Pickett is our guest," Hetherington said sternly. "We're not going to make her work like a navvy. She can keep to her room until the package is well on its way. Between the two of us, you and I can handle things, at least until you reach town."

Flynn shrugged, seemingly taking Hetherington's scold with a good grace. "Aye, I don't doubt I can find any number o' lads workin' on Nelson's Pillar who wouldn't object to a job a bit more to their likin'. Once we're after finishin' at the castle, we can take care of the wharves and be back in Sackville Street in time for 'em to collect their wages."

Julia was careful not to betray any sort of interest in their conversation, but her mind was awhirl. The fact that Flynn intended to hire transport seemed to indicate that she was right in thinking there were no horses in the stables; apparently the ones that had pulled the carriage that had brought her here had also been hired. By Bohannan, perhaps? And what sort of "package" required not only a wagon and team to deliver it, but five or more men—Flynn, Hetherington, and Flynn's "few lads"—to load it? One thing was certain: she would discover nothing by keeping meekly to her room.

"If my help is needed, I don't mind—" she began, only to be cut off by Hetherington.

"Now, now, Mrs. Pickett, you won't want to muss your pretty dress. We can't have your husband coming and seeing you looking like a chimney sweep, now, do we?"

As she had been wearing her "pretty dress" for more than

a se'ennight, as near as she could tell, Julia thought there was very little she could do to it to make it look worse than it already did. But what was in the package that might leave her looking like a chimney sweep? Coal, perhaps? She thought the Irish used peat for fuel. Did it leave the same black smudges? She had no idea, and didn't even know what questions to ask that they might be willing to answer.

"If I set out at first light," Flynn continued, "I can be after hirin' a wagon and team and returnin' by noon. We can be loadin' the package and then deliverin' it to Dublin first thing the next mornin'."

Hetherington scowled fiercely at him. "I can't possibly go in two days! What if Mr. Pickett should arrive and find me absent?"

If delivery must wait until John's arrival, Julia thought with some satisfaction, *then the people of Dublin will be awaiting their package for a very long time.* For he must surely have received her message by now, and turned back. Curiously enough, it never occurred to her to think that perhaps he had lost the scent, and was searching for her in quite the wrong place—the Lake District, perhaps, where he and Hetherington had first crossed paths. No, he would certainly trace her as far as Dublin, where he would be warned not to pursue her.

One thing was certain: with Flynn gone, she and Hetherington would be alone in the house from early morning until noon. If she could contrive to escape from the house unseen, she might even be able to outrun the much older man, should he spy her from one of the windows and give chase.

Tomorrow it must be, then. She would never have a better opportunity.

17

In Which John Pickett and His Brother-in-Law
Make a Surprising Discovery

H ere!" Jamie called to the driver, rapping on the roof of the carriage to make sure he was heard. "Set us down here."

The jarvey obliged, but cast a dubious eye about at his surroundings. Night would be falling soon, and there were no houses, no buildings at all, only trees and dry-stone walls zigzagging up and down the rolling hills, enclosing fields where recently shorn sheep grazed. Nor were there any sounds of human habitation, nothing but the chirrup of nocturnal insects interrupted by the occasional bleat of the sheep or the disapproving snort of one of his horses. He was inclined to agree with the horse.

"There's nothing here," he pointed out to the man who appeared to be the leader of the four passengers—a military man, or used to be, unless he missed his guess. "It'll soon be nightfall, and where will you be then?"

"In the dark, I suppose," Jamie said with a smile. "But there's still enough of a moon to see by, so we'll rub along well enough."

The jarvey shrugged and let the fellow have his way. As soon as the last man had disembarked, he flicked his whip over his leader's flanks, and the carriage moved away.

"Well, I like that," Carson said in a voice that conveyed just the opposite. "How the devil are we supposed to get back to the village?"

"We walk," Jamie said, starting off down a weed-choked drive.

"*Walk!*" complained Carson, scrambling to catch up with the other three. "But it must be five miles!"

"It's less than four," said Pickett, who would gladly have trudged twice that distance to rescue Julia. "I can tell you're on the Horse Patrol. The Foot can walk that far by noon," he added, having spent five years of his life with that organization before his promotion to principal officer.

"Buck up, Mr. Carson," Jamie chided. "In the army, it's not unusual to march twenty miles in a day."

"I thought you were in the cavalry," said Carson, not at all placated.

"I was," Jamie conceded with a nod. "For thirteen years. On two occasions, my horse was shot out from under me, and on a third, the brute took fright, unseated me, and bolted. Believe me, I was just happy to get out of there with a whole skin, never mind the walk! Now, since the secret of a successful reconnaissance lies in not being discovered, I suggest we stubble the small talk."

Since Carson was the one doing most of the talking, it was very clear for whom this warning was intended. Much as Pickett enjoyed the spectacle of Harry Carson being put in his place, he was too impatient to reach Julia to savor the moment as he otherwise might have done. He glanced at Jamie and gave him a grateful nod. This was why he had fetched his brother-in-law in the first place: to plan the rescue mission and see to its execution when he himself was too distraught to think clearly.

Now that the moment was at hand, however, Pickett found that his mind had never been sharper. He stopped and pointed down at the ground, then looked up to make sure his companions saw and understood. The drive was badly overgrown, but the long grasses had been bent and broken as if crushed beneath carriage wheels, or horses' hooves, or both. Someone had passed this way recently, and very likely more than once. Jamie and Carson both nodded. Thomas merely looked confused, but he had the wisdom not to ask for enlightenment.

Pickett, taking pity on him, put his hand on his valet's shoulder and leaned in close to his ear to whisper, "Someone's been here. See how the grass is bent?"

Thomas nodded in belated understanding, and the four resumed their trek. At last they rounded a curve and topped a hill, and beheld a house in the middle distance, a large, stately house of gray stone. As they drew nearer, keeping to the trees for cover, signs of neglect here, too, became clear. The roof was missing its shingles in places, and although the last rays of the sun were reflected in most of the windows, the absence of any reflection in others betrayed the fact that the glass panes had been broken out. A light burned in one of the windows on the ground floor, and another one on the floor above.

Even as Pickett's brain registered this fact, a female figure moved to the upper window and drew a curtain across it, cutting off all but the faintest sliver of light. *Julia!*

He must have made some instinctive move in her direction, for Jamie grasped his sleeve and mouthed a single word: *Tomorrow.*

Pickett nodded, making note of that window's position relative to the others. At least he knew where to look for her if—no, *when* they gained access to the house.

"At least we know they don't have her chained up in some attic or cellar," Jamie leaned close to whisper. "That might be useful to know, if we should have to fire the house and smoke them out."

A knot formed in Pickett's stomach at the idea of setting fire to the house with Julia inside. For all they knew, she might be locked inside that room, and Hetherington and company might decide to cut their losses, letting the fire destroy any evidence of their crimes. The end result—Julia's death—would be the same. With any luck, they would be able to rescue her without resorting to such a tactic. Well, they would just have to, Pickett thought, setting his jaw. The alternative was unthinkable.

After that, there was very little they could do until the house was dark, indicating that all the occupants were abed. Even after the last light was extinguished, Jamie made no move to emerge from the trees. They sat silently in the gathering darkness for perhaps half an hour (although it seemed to Pickett like they'd been waiting for most of the day), then Jamie opened the haversack he carried and removed two dark lanterns. Turning so that his body would prevent any light from being seen from the house, he lit the two lanterns and adjusted their shutters so that they emitted a narrow sliver of light just sufficient to allow the bearers to walk safely without running into a tree or falling over a cliff.

Jamie handed one of the lanterns to Pickett and the other to Carson, then reached into the bag again and withdrew four pistols. These were no surprise to Pickett, as they had been discussed extensively before the men set out on their mission. Thomas's pistol wasn't loaded, for he had never been taught how to use a firearm, and Jamie intended to take no chances.

"But they won't know that," he'd assured the valet. "Most men who find themselves staring down the barrel of a gun aren't going to stop and ask questions."

The other three pistols were all primed and loaded, but Jamie's instructions had been clear. "Don't shoot unless it becomes absolutely necessary," he'd told both Pickett and Carson. "Remember, letting off firearms will only serve to rouse the house, and we don't yet know how many men are inside."

As he gave each man his weapon, Jamie fixed his comrades-in-arms with an intense look that served to remind them of his instructions without his having to say a word. Once they were all armed, he motioned for Carson and Thomas to circle the house clockwise, while he and Pickett took the other direction. Pickett received his orders with some misgivings. Wasn't it supposed to be bad luck to circle a building counterclockwise? Widdershins, as it had been called in the days before clocks had been invented. Or did that only apply to circling a church, like Burd Ellen in the fairy tale? More to the point, why was his brain fixed on such insignificant details when Julia was only a few hundred feet away, and every step he took brought him nearer to her.

Slowly, carefully, they approached the house, Pickett holding the shuttered lantern low so that it illuminated only the ground before their feet. The sky was fully dark by now, and the house a great black bulk rising sharply on their left. When they reached the place below the window where he'd seen Julia, Pickett held the light for just a moment on a small patch of pebbles, any one of which would have been the perfect size for lobbing at her window.

"*Tomorrow.*"

Jamie's whisper was scarcely more than a breath at his ear. Pickett sighed, nodded, and moved on. No one stepped out of the shadows to challenge them, and he began to hope that perhaps there were not so many of them, after all. In addition to Hetherington himself, there would be at least two—the man who had seized Julia, and the driver of the vehicle that had spirited her and her abductor away—but perhaps few, if any, more. Certainly there was no evidence of a small army of Irishmen determined to pursue independence by any means at hand, including the abduction of an innocent woman. Then again, Hetherington's unstable mental state made him as dangerously unpredictable as any number of men under his command.

They had rounded the end of the house by this time, and a dark shape some distance away on the right indicated the presence of an outbuilding. Jamie nudged Pickett's arm and pointed in that direction, a gesture which Pickett interpreted to mean they should investigate it. Fighting the irrational feeling that he was somehow abandoning Julia, he turned and positioned the lantern to light their way.

The double doors were wide enough to drive a carriage through, suggesting that the building was—or had been at some time in the past—a carriage house or a stable, or perhaps both. And yet the odors usually associated with horses were absent: no smell of oats or hay, no stench of manure. If horses were still kept here, it wasn't often, or for very long.

Jamie reached for one of the doors to pull it open, but it wouldn't yield. Pickett risked opening the lantern's shutter a bit wider, and saw that, instead of the bar and staples one might expect to see on a farm building, this one had been fitted with the sort of lock usually found inside a house. Wordlessly, Pickett handed the lantern to Jamie, then fumbled in the inside pocket of his brown serge coat for the hairpin he'd kept there since his marriage in case of just such an exigency. Unlike Harry Carson, Jamie had prior knowledge of his brother-in-law's unique talent, having once won a tidy sum by wagering on it even before he'd seen a demonstration. In view of that experience, he was not surprised when, seconds after Pickett dropped to one knee, the wide door swung open, groaning slightly on its hinges.

Pistols at the ready, Pickett and Jamie slipped inside,

opening the door only as far as was absolutely necessary lest the creaking of the hinges betray their presence. Once within, Jamie pulled the door closed behind them and Pickett opened the shutter and held the lantern high. As he'd suspected, there were no horses, no animals of any kind, and no carriages. In fact, the cavernous building appeared to be empty except for a collection of sacks, crates, and barrels.

"What have we here?" Jamie asked softly. He engaged the safety catch of his pistol and shoved it into the waistband of his breeches, then withdrew a knife from his coat pocket and cut a slit in one of the sacks. Fine black powder spilled out in a steady stream.

A knot began to form in the pit of Pickett's belly as he watched the little pile forming on the ground at Jamie's feet. "Is that—"

"Unless I miss my guess—" Jamie shifted the sack to cease the flow, then knelt to scoop up a little of the spillage in his hand. He sniffed it, then let it fall back to the ground and dusted the remains from his hands. It left black smudges behind. "Gunpowder. It looks like your friend is planning quite a party."

"My God," breathed Pickett.

Julia was being held captive in what was essentially a powder magazine.

Rescuing her had just become a lot more difficult.

And a lot more dangerous.

18

In Which Julia Attempts an Escape

W hatever we do, we keep him—them—away from that stable," Jamie said softly, peering over the tops of the cards in his hands to address the little group seated around the table in the taproom of Summerhill's only public house.

They had claimed the table nearest the fireplace, as the crackling of the fire in the grate—necessary for both light and heat so far north, even in mid-July—provided them with some cover, should any of their fellow guests have a penchant for eavesdropping. Even so, they spoke in hushed tones, raising their voices only to indicate reaction to the card game in progress.

Granted, all this secrecy might be unnecessary; their reconnaissance had seemed to indicate that Hetherington had very few allies who might be amongst them at that very minute, fortifying themselves with Mr. Guinness's finest. Still, it was quite possible that the locals would be quick to throw their support behind any plot claiming Irish independence as its goal, if some careless word on their part should betray the fact that such a plot existed. Better, surely, to err on the side of caution and present themselves as nothing more than four visiting Englishmen enjoying a friendly game of whist.

"One stray bullet could blow the building and anyone inside it to perdition," Jamie continued, punctuating this statement by playing the king of hearts.

Pickett groaned, a supposed reaction to his opponent's move that was only partially feigned.

Carson, having nothing more promising in his hand, tossed down a three and asked, "How are we to do that? Keep this fellow and his cohorts away from the stable, I mean?"

"You and Thomas said there was a door on the end of the house opposite the stables," Jamie reminded him, as Thomas discarded. "The three of us will take up a position some little distance from it and make enough noise to draw Hetherington out—not so much as to be obvious, mind you. Just three men who are trying to carry out a stealth attack and not making a very good show of it."

Carson frowned. "I should have thought that would have exactly the opposite effect, and make him escape through any of the other doors."

"There's always the chance he'll try to outflank us," Jamie acknowledged. "But I think it's unlikely."

"Why?" Thomas asked, then hastily added, "Begging your pardon, sir."

"Because that's a maneuver you use when a frontal assault would fail. You count on an element of surprise to make up for being outmanned, or outgunned. But Hetherington has, or thinks he has, an advantage that we can't hope to match."

"Oh?" Carson asked. "And what's that? What good will his arsenal do him if he has to go through us to reach it?"

"A good point, Mr. Carson, but that's not the advantage I was talking about." Jamie cast a sympathetic glance at his brother-in-law. "He has another."

"A hostage," Pickett said in a hollow voice. "As long as he's got Julia, he holds the upper hand—and he knows it." Hence the severed finger, as a reminder to Pickett of just how powerless he was.

"Which is why," Jamie continued, picking up the thread of his narrative, "While we're keeping Hetherington busy on one end of the house, Mr. Pickett will approach from the other end, slip inside through the front door, go upstairs, and fetch Julia. Once he's got her out of the house and away to a place of safety, he'll come back and lend whatever reinforcements may—"

"Look here," Carson interrupted, "it seems to me that we're going about this all wrong."

"Oh?" Far from taking offense, Jamie seemed genuinely interested in hearing Carson's objections. "In what way?"

"You're going on the assumption that Hetherington can't guard both Mrs. Pickett and his explosives at the same time, but what if he *can?* What I mean is, we know he has at least two men working for him; what if one or both of them surprise Mr. Pickett on the stairs, or some such thing? Then Hetherington still has his hostage, and we've got no reinforcements coming."

Jamie sighed. "Your point is a valid one, Mr. Carson, and I'm sorry I can't give you a better answer. It would be nice if we could know for sure exactly how many men we'll be facing, but we can't. We just have to do the best we can with the information we've got. If Mr. Pickett should find himself in a tight spot, then I'm sure he'll think of something."

Carson regarded Pickett doubtfully. "You'll forgive me for not being filled with confidence."

Pickett had been studying the cards in his hand, but at this slight to his powers of improvisation he looked up, bristling.

Jamie laid a restraining hand on his arm, but addressed himself to Harry. "If there's one thing I learned in the army, Mr. Carson, it's that the most careful plan of attack falls apart within minutes of battle being joined. The better part of warfare consists of making it up as you go along. And you won't find many better at it than this fellow here."

"Thank you, brother mine," Pickett said, then played his ace and took the trick.

* * *

Julia sat alone with her host and captor at breakfast, facing him down the length of the dining room table and trying to act as if plotting an escape were the last thing on her mind. Of Flynn there was no sign; had he already left on his errand, she wondered, or was there some other explanation for his absence? The image of Bohannan as she had last seen him rose unbidden to her mind, the big body, so recently alive, sprawled on the drawing room floor in an ungainly heap, all because he had spoken up in her defense . . .

Stop it, she told herself firmly. *You need to be keeping a clear head and gathering information, not dwelling on horrors.* Aloud, she said, "How fresh the scones are this morning! Mr. Flynn will be sorry to have missed them."

"Ah, but you're wrong there, Mrs. Pickett," Hetherington informed her. "He didn't miss them at all. He set off on an errand at first light, and his wife made them early enough that he could have a couple before he left. In fact, you might say we're making do with Flynn's leavings."

"Is it his wife who has been cooking our meals, then? I had wondered." This was true so far as it went, although her speculations had usually centered on wondering whether the cook might be disposed to sympathize with her own plight, and whether this person lived on the premises or only came as day labor from the village—Summerhill, Flynn had once called it before Hetherington had shushed him into silence. She had pretended not to notice, but had filed the name of the nearest hamlet away in her brain; it might be useful, when she escaped, to know something of what lay beyond her immediate surroundings. "I should like to go down to the kitchen and offer Mrs. Flynn my compliments, if you have no objection."

He gave a bark of laughter. "I have no objection to you going to the kitchen whenever you like, but you won't find Mrs. Flynn there."

"Oh?" Julia prompted. "And why is that?"

He picked up his coffee cup and took a sip, and for a moment Julia wondered if she had pushed him too hard. Then he shrugged. "Her man was going to town today, and she wanted to go with him."

Town, Julia thought. *Not "the village," but "town."* Presumably, that meant Dublin, where the package (whatever it was) was to be delivered. But he was only going as far as Summerhill, surely, to hire a wagon and carthorses—wasn't he? The answer would determine how long she would have before he returned. She wished she could remember exactly what he'd said; it wouldn't do to overestimate her window of opportunity and thus let her best chance go to waste.

Aloud, she merely said, "Perhaps he should take her to town more often, if it inspires her to such culinary heights. I could become accustomed to having these for breakfast every morning."

As if in proof of this statement, she reached for another scone. In fact, she needed an excuse for making a heartier breakfast than usual. If she were to take advantage of Flynn's absence and make her escape, it might be some time before she had the opportunity—to say nothing of the food—to eat again. And yet she'd eaten little since her abduction; now she needed an explanation ready to hand, should Hetherington wonder at her improved appetite.

But Hetherington, it soon transpired, was occupied with thoughts of his own. As Julia pushed back her chair and rose from the table, he spoke.

"A word of caution, Mrs. Pickett, before you go. I would be obliged to you if you would keep to your room today."

Julia had no intention of keeping to her room today, of all days, but she judged it wise to keep this observation to herself. Still, accepting this dictum too meekly would surely arouse his suspicions just as much as outright defiance would have done.

"You said I might go down to the kitchens," she reminded him.

"Aye, when you said you wished to speak to Mrs. Flynn. But since you won't find her there, why bother to go at all?"

"May I not walk about the grounds, then?" she asked, knowing quite well what the answer would be.

"Not today, my dear. Perhaps tomorrow, if your husband hasn't come by then."

Once again, his voice was that of an indulgent uncle gently reproving a favorite niece. Anyone would find it impossible to believe that he was mad—anyone who hadn't seen him shoot Bohannan in the back . . .

"Very well, then," she said, not daring to offer further protest. "I shall choose a book from the library, and spend the day reading."

Julia tended to avoid the library, as it was an unpleasant room. It reeked of dry rot from cracks in the ceiling, while in one corner the blackened walls bore witness to some long-ago fire; apparently its long vacancy had been interrupted at intervals by vagrants taking up temporary residence. She stopped at the bookshelf nearest the door and selected a mildewed volume at random, then returned with it to the bedchamber that had been allotted to her on the day she'd arrived. How many days had it been? She supposed it didn't really matter, just so long as today was the last.

Once inside the room, she set the book on her bedside

table and promptly forgot all about it. She locked the door, hoping to delay as long as possible the moment Hetherington, or Flynn, or both, realized she was no longer in her room. She crossed the floor to the window, and twitched back the curtain just enough to see through. Her room overlooked the front of the house, and so offered no view of the stable; at the moment, all was quiet, at least so far as she could see. Still, she forced herself to wait long enough to allay any suspicions Hetherington might have that she was not reading in her room, exactly as she said she would be.

The stillness was broken by the tinny chime of a clock somewhere in the house. Julia could not recall seeing a clock, but then, she had not explored the entire house. She had not noticed the sound before, but then, the house was quieter now that only she and Hetherington were in residence. Had it been chiming all along, and she had simply not heard, or had Hetherington only wound it today, finding it important to the execution of his mission? She wondered how long that neglected clock had continued to mark the hours for a family who was no longer there, until it finally fell silent for want of a hand to wind it. She would wait until the next chime, she decided, and then she would make her escape from this house with its tragic past and its terrifying future.

Some time later, she heard the discordant notes of the Whittington chimes—discordant because they were badly out of tune—followed by the clock's striking the hour.

It was time.

Julia took off her shoes lest the sound of her footsteps in the quiet house betray her. She dared not try to slip down the stairs to the front door; she suspected Hetherington would be quick to discover any such attempt on her part, no matter how complacent he might have appeared at the breakfast table. Fortunately, the dilapidated condition of the house had revealed another possible escape route. The paper was peeling from the walls, and the resulting gaps revealed the narrow jib door through which servants would have gained access to the room in more prosperous days. Beyond this door would be a staircase descending two floors to the kitchens. And from the kitchens, one might reach the service door—and beyond it, freedom.

Julia lingered only long enough to light her bedside candle, then picked up her shoes and candle, opened the jib door (grimacing at the faint protest of long-unused hinges), and started down the stairs. She eased the door closed behind her and was glad she had remembered to provide herself with the candle; without it, the darkness would have been complete. The stairs were narrow and uncarpeted, and she groped her way down one tread at a time, clinging to the handrail with one hand and her candlestick with the other. Alas, this left no hand to hold her shoes, so she was obliged to pause long enough to stuff them into her bodice before resuming her journey.

Once or twice she heard something skittering in the dark, but aside from these unsettling reminders that she and Hetherington were not entirely alone in the house (for they apparently had plenty of four-footed companions), her escape from her prison was surprisingly uneventful. No one waited in the kitchen to demand where she was going, and when she put a tentative hand to the service door and pushed it open, no one lurked on the other side, ready to raise a hue and cry.

With a sigh that was equal parts triumph and relief, she braced against the doorframe for balance while she put on her shoes, then set out for the long drive that would take her to the road. She could almost feel hostile eyes upon her, watching her from the house, and the copse of trees that would eventually shield her from view now seemed a hundred miles away. She was sorely tempted to set out instead across the neglected fields, but with no landmarks to guide her, she might walk for days without reaching any village or hamlet where she might seek help. Then, too, there was the fact that the back of the house had tall windows overlooking a crumbling stone terrace; if Hetherington were still in the dining room, or had repaired to the drawing room after breakfast, he could not fail to see her. No, risky as it was, the front of the house and the drive leading to the road were still the better option.

Having made her decision, Julia refused to waste time or energy in questioning it—until she reached the end of the house nearest the stable. She recalled again the sacks and barrels stored there, and Flynn's determination to close the gaping door before she could see what was inside. There might have been a horse just out of her view, she reasoned, perhaps even more than one; Flynn hadn't allowed her the chance to find out. But there was no one to stop her now, and if there chanced to be a saddle horse in the stable, then the fact that she could ride would more than make up for the time she would lose.

Her mind made up, she crept stealthily toward the stable, inwardly chiding herself for taking an unnecessary risk. *Admit it, what you really want is to discover what it is, this package that is to be delivered to Dublin.* She could not forget Flynn's mention of "finishing" something at the castle. Hetherington's name had been linked with a castle once before, and had it not been for John's intervention, the results might have been disastrous. She reached the stable door and, finding it unlocked (no doubt in preparation for Flynn's return), she pushed it open. She slipped inside and paused for a moment, allowing her eyes to adjust to the dim light.

Just as she had suspected, there were no horses to be found. She strode up to the pile of sacks. A bit had been spilled on the floor, and three parallel grooves indicated where someone had attempted to scoop it up with his fingers. Julia knelt down and followed suit, rubbing the gritty black substance between her thumb and forefinger. No daughter of that avid sportsman, Sir Thaddeus Runyon, could fail to recognize gunpowder when she saw it. Whatever Hetherington's plans for Dublin were, they involved firepower—and plenty of it. She had to escape, not only for her own sake, but in order to warn someone—anyone!—of what was in store for the city if he and Flynn had their way.

She started for the door—and froze as a shadow fell across the opening. Someone was out there.

And she was trapped inside.

19

*In Which Mr. and Mrs. John Pickett Are Reunited,
Albeit under Less Than Ideal Circumstances*

P ickett left Jamie, Carson, and Thomas concealed in the copse of trees overlooking the end of the house opposite the stable. Running at a crouch, he crossed the stretch of open ground until he reached the house, then pressed himself flat against the wall with his back to the weathered gray stone so as not to be visible from any of the windows. With pistol drawn, he worked his way around to the front door, stooping low whenever he had to pass in front of one of the tall windows. He had almost reached the door when he glimpsed a movement out of the corner of his eye. He whirled about, aiming his pistol, only to let out a sigh of relief at the discovery that it had only been the stable door, now standing slightly ajar. *Only the wind,* he thought, scolding himself for his overstretched nerves.

But no, the door had been locked when he and Jamie had discovered the cache of explosives. Either someone had been extremely careless, or someone was inside. Hetherington might be mad as a March hare, but not even the man's worst enemy—which, Pickett supposed, was him—could call the fellow careless. Someone was inside, then, someone who might choose to exit the stable just in time to see him spiriting Julia out of the house.

Pickett wrestled with indecision, but only for a moment. Whoever was in the stable, it would surely be better to confront them now, alone, before they could raise the alarm. At best, he would eliminate a potential threat before it could become a real one; at worst, he might be killed before he ever reached Julia. But with Pickett himself dead, Hetherington might even free her. After all, he had no particular grudge against Julia; it was the prospect of seeing his enemy suffer that now drove the man.

Dropping once more into a stooping run, Pickett approached the stable, pausing at the door to listen for any sounds coming from inside. All was quiet except for the pounding of his own heart. He peered cautiously around the door. The cache of black powder was still there, but between him and it stood a disheveled woman in a torn and dirty gown, staring at the stable door with wide, frightened eyes. She was the most beautiful thing he'd ever seen in his life.

"Julia!"

He'd spoken softly so as not to startle her, but her reaction astounded him. As he stole inside and pulled the door closed behind him, she took a step backward, holding out one hand as if to ward off a blow. "Oh, no! Oh, nonono!"

He froze where he stood. "Sweetheart? Do you not know

me?" If she didn't, if Hetherington's treatment of her had deprived her of her wits, then he would die in the slowest, most agonizing manner Pickett could contrive.

She blinked at him in bewilderment. "Of course I know you! How could I not? But I—I told you not to come. I left a letter for you."

"Yes, I know. I got it." A little smile touched his lips. "I've never read such a great piece of nonsense in all my life."

"It's true," she insisted. "It's not me he wants; it's you. He knew you would come for me."

"And yet you thought you had only to explain the matter to me, and I would turn around and go back home," he chided gently. "Is it possible that Hetherington knows me better than you do?"

"No." Even as she spoke the word, she knew why it was that she'd taken so much time in plotting her escape. She had told herself she was being cautious, but in fact, she'd been anticipating his arrival every bit as confidently as Hetherington had done. "John, I—I felt the baby move. I didn't feel quite so alone anymore. It was almost like you were there—here—with me."

He nodded, but in so distracted a manner that it was clear his thoughts were elsewhere. "That's—that's good. Julia, I'm going to get you out of here, but first I have to know—did he—harm you—in any way?"

She didn't have to ask what he meant. "No—that is, Flynn struck me on the head in order to get me out of the house, but I promise you I haven't been—that is—neither Hetherington nor either of his men—they—they didn't—"

"Sweetheart, no one could do anything to you that would make me love you less," he assured her. "I just need to know how slowly he ought to die."

She gave a shaky little laugh. "John, don't talk like that! You're frightening me."

"You don't think I will avenge any mistreatment you've suffered?" If she'd had any doubt of it, his tone and the expression on his face would have been enough to inform her otherwise.

"No, no, pray don't! I couldn't bear to see you become like him, obsessed with vengeance and eaten up with hatred— I couldn't bear it! But if that isn't it—John, will you not even touch me?"

"I've spent the last four days not knowing if you were dead or alive," Pickett said, his voice shaking. "If I touch you now, I might not be able to let you go, and Hetherington would come and find me here sobbing over you like a blubbering fool."

"I'm willing to risk it, if you are." Suddenly her face crumpled. "Please—I've been so frightened—"

And suddenly she was in his arms, and he was kissing her and murmuring endearments into her ear and calling her his brave, clever girl for thinking to warn him in a coded message, and then kissing her some more, in between words that made no sense.

"—Should have known—so sorry—ought to have— warned you—"

"John?" She drew back slightly in order to look him in the face. "Darling, what are you talking about?"

"He threatened you—that day in the Lake District. He told me he would come for you someday, after I'd let down my guard."

"That was why you wanted me to go to Mama and Papa while you were away," she said thoughtfully, recalling their conversation on the day he'd told her he was being sent to Dunbury.

"I didn't like leaving you alone, although at the time I didn't know—I'm so sorry—"

She pressed her fingers to his lips, cutting off another round of apologies. "Nonsense! Why should you have warned me about something that was unlikely to occur? For all we knew, he had already been executed."

But Pickett refused to receive absolution. "I knew he hadn't. I asked Mr. Colquhoun to let me know when the thing was done, and he hadn't said a word on the subject. I didn't want you to worry—"

"So instead, you've spent the last month worrying about it yourself, all alone."

Her tone was pitying, not accusatory; clearly, it behooved him to bring her to some recognition of his sins. "I thought it was the right thing to do, but Claudia said—"

"*Claudia?* What has she to do with this?"

"When I got word that you'd been abducted—Mr. Colquhoun sent a courier to Dunbury with the news—I went to fetch Jamie. I needed a plan, and I couldn't seem to think—"

"Yes, I see it now," she said, nodding slowly. "John, recollect that Claudia spent thirteen years hiding from a dangerous man who was very much alive, and free. It would be imperative that she know as much as possible about where he was, or what he was doing, at any given time. But this was different. You had every reason to believe that Robert Hetherington was locked up awaiting the assizes. To imagine otherwise would merely be borrowing trouble—and so I would have told you, if you had chosen to confide in me."

"Then—you think I did the right thing in not telling you?" he asked, almost afraid to hope.

"Oh, no," she said, smiling up at him. "I think you should have told me—but only so that you would not have borne such a burden alone. That's what marriage is, you know—or what it ought to be."

In answer, he took her hands in his and pressed a kiss onto the tip of each finger with an intensity that surprised her.

"John? What are you doing?"

"Counting them," was his rather cryptic reply.

"What?" she asked, utterly bewildered.

"Never mind."

Having completed this exercise (and, presumably, arriving at the correct number), he took her arm and gave her a little tug toward the door. "I think we'd better be going. If I'm going to have to confront Hetherington, I'd just as soon not do it here, in the middle of a powder magazine."

Relieved as he was to be reunited with his wife, Pickett was not so lost to the dangers of their situation as to forget all caution. He withdrew the pistol from the waistband of his breeches—he couldn't remember at exactly what point he had put it there, but he was glad to see he had at least engaged the safety catch, else he might have accidentally put a serious damper on their reunion—then thumbed the catch free and crossed the stable floor with her hand held tightly in his. He paused before the door and listened for any sounds from outside. Finding none, he pushed it open with the nose of his pistol and leaned out to peer around the door. No one moved. Although he knew there were at least three men—his own confederates—on the other end of the house, he and Julia might have been alone on the neglected estate, for all the evidence to the contrary.

"Let's go," he said, lowering his voice to a near whisper.

They had scarcely emerged from the stable when a familiar figure stepped away from the corner of the house, an elderly man whose pistol hand was nevertheless steady as he aimed his weapon at Julia.

"I've been expecting you, Mr. Pickett." Hetherington's tone was pleasant, like that of a host welcoming a long-awaited guest, but the light of madness burned in his eyes. "Once again, Patrick Colquhoun's *enfant prodige* fails to live up to his reputation. Stupid boy! I might have shot you at any time as you crossed the lawn."

"Then why didn't you?" Pickett's voice was cool as he released Julia's hand and would have given her a little nudge, putting himself between her and his adversary, but the twitch of Hetherington's pistol hand advised against such a move.

"Because it would have been too easy a death for you," Hetherington pointed out impatiently, as if this should have been obvious. "First you shall have to endure the agony of seeing your wife slain before your eyes, as I did. Now, you will oblige me by dropping your weapon."

Having no other alternative, Pickett held his pistol out to his side and let it fall to the ground. The gesture left him feeling naked and exposed. "Let her go, Hetherington. Your quarrel is with me, not my wife."

His adversary nodded, exclaiming delightedly, "That's it, Mr. Pickett! Beg for mercy, plead with me to spare her!"

Pickett understood the words to be rhetorical, but when he showed no inclination to follow orders, Hetherington's face turned red with rage, and the hand holding his pistol shook menacingly. "I said, *beg*, damn you!"

Pickett swallowed hard. "Please, please don't do this," he implored, more than a little disturbed by how easy it was to debase himself, knowing all the while that it would make no difference in the end. "You're a better man than this—"

"On your knees!" When Pickett would have obeyed this new command, gauging at the same time whether it would bring his pistol within reach, Hetherington realized his error and abruptly changed his mind. "No, don't! Stay on your feet!"

"Please—" Pickett began, but Hetherington's disturbed mind had already moved on to other things.

"You have a confederate, do you not? At least one, and quite possibly more, if the footprints I found in the stable this morning are anything to judge by. You will invite them to join us, and tell them to leave their weapons behind."

Footprints, Pickett thought miserably. His own and Jamie's footprints, clearly visible on the stable's dirt floor. He couldn't blame his brother-in-law for not thinking to eradicate this telltale evidence of their clandestine visit—it had been Major Pennington's responsibility in the army to lead cavalry charges, not reconnaissance missions—but he must certainly blame himself. How could he have been so careless? He supposed it was some combination of the darkness, and the feeble light from the lantern, and the fact that he'd just caught a glimpse of Julia in one of the upstairs windows of the house. None of which excused the fact that he ought to have taken such a precaution, and had not.

But there was no time for self-recriminations. Hetherington, having given his orders, was waiting impatiently for them to be obeyed. Pickett had to summon at least one of his allies to walk unarmed and unsuspecting into a confrontation from which he might not escape alive. Granted, Hetherington could only fire his pistol once, but thanks to his stockpile of ammunition, he could kill the lot of them without firing a shot; he had only to herd them all into the stable and set off the powder.

"*Call them!*" Hetherington shouted, waving the pistol he still held aimed at Julia's head.

Call who? Pickett thought frantically. He would have preferred to leave Jamie free to design some plan for their rescue, but aside from the fact that his brother-in-law, however capable, could not work miracles, there was the fact that it was Jamie's footprints, along with Pickett's, that Hetherington had discovered in the stable. Would he take the time to compare the prints to the feet of the man who came in answer to Pickett's summons? Pickett thought it unlikely, but then, who could predict the actions of a madman? No, he would have to summon Jamie, and Thomas as well, since Hetherington suspected more than one, and trust to Harry Carson's ingenuity. He only hoped Carson was up to the task.

"Jamie! Thomas!" His gaze never wavered from Hetherington as he raised his voice. "Leave your weapons and come here!"

After a brief, expectant silence, two men emerged from around the rear corner of the house only to check at the sight of Pickett, disarmed and helpless, and Julia, staring down the barrel of a pistol.

"Don't be shy, gentlemen," Hetherington chided. "Come and join us! You're just in time to witness an execution."

He waited with barely contained impatience as the new arrivals slowly made their way to the little group standing on the bare patch of ground before the stable. Their hands were empty, Pickett noted; he'd been hoping that Jamie would somehow surmise what had happened, and would ignore that particular behest.

"Now that we're all here," Hetherington continued, turning back to Pickett, "have you any last words for your wife before I kill her?"

It was now or never. Pickett raised his hands to the level of his shoulders in a gesture of surrender, then, after one uncertain glance at his adversary, turned slightly toward Julia and lowered himself very slowly to one knee. "My lady," he addressed her with great formality, "if you could so far demean yourself as to agree to bestow upon me your hand in marriage, I promise I will do my utmost to see that you,"—his voice shook slightly—"that you will never live to regret it."

"Oh, John," she breathed, and it seemed to Pickett as if all the stars in the heavens shone from her eyes. "I'd rather have four months with you than forty years with anyone else."

"Well, I like that!" grumbled Harry Carson, emerging from the front corner of the house. "I suppose the three of you have been having a fine time, while I—"

Pickett lunged for his pistol. Immediately Hetherington's gun was trained on him.

"I said drop it!" he shrieked, his face contorted with rage.

But the balance of power had shifted. Now that Julia was no longer the immediate target, Pickett was willing to take chances he would not have risked before. For the second time, he held the pistol out to his side, but instead of letting it fall, he looked Robert Hetherington squarely in the eye and fired—not at his adversary, but straight through the gaping door into the stable.

And then everything happened at once. A second gunshot followed the first in quick succession. Pickett grabbed Julia's arm and dragged her to the ground, flinging himself on top of her.

"*Nooo!*" Hetherington screamed, throwing down his weapon as he ran through the stable door into the darkness beyond.

"*Get down!*" Pickett shouted, and in the next instant the building erupted in flame, raining splinters and straw down onto his back.

He wasn't sure how long he lay there, shielding his wife with his own body. He supposed it could not have been more than a minute, two at the most, but it seemed like an eternity before he rose stiffly to his feet and held out a hand to assist her.

"You're all right?" he said breathlessly. "I didn't hurt you?"

"No, but"—she glanced toward the burning stable, or what was left of it—"John, he—"

"Shouldn't we—I don't know—try to find him, sir?" Thomas, slower to react than the others and as a consequence blown off his feet by the blast, picked himself up and dusted himself off.

"I doubt there'll be much to find," Jamie said, raking his fingers through his hair to rid it of any burning cinders. "A timely arrival, Mr. Carson. Well done."

"Yes—I'm obliged to you, Harry." Pickett looked up from brushing smoldering embers from Julia's skirt. "Julia, this is Harry Carson of the Horse Patrol. Harry—my wife, Mrs. Pickett."

Julia extended her hand. "How do you do, Mr. Carson? I'm sorry we should have to meet under such circumstances, but given the outcome, I can't complain. I don't like to think about what might have happened if you hadn't distracted Mr. Hetherington when you did."

Even in her disheveled condition, Julia was a far cry from the wealthy, middle-aged woman Carson had envisioned. He supposed he ought to tell her that his appearance on the scene had been nothing more than a happy accident, that he'd resented being left out of whatever action had apparently taken place, since firearms were no longer needed. But his prowess with the fairer sex seemed to have deserted him, and

he could do no more than stare at the lady and stammer, "I—
I—I—"

"I daresay the neighbors will soon see the smoke and
come to offer assistance in putting the fire out, or at least
stopping it from spreading," Jamie said, eyeing the heap of
burning boards and splintered beams. "I think we'd better
agree on what, and how much, to tell them about what took
place here."

"Flynn is still free!" Julia exclaimed in sudden
recollection. "Bohannan is dead—Mr. Hetherington shot him
when he spoke up in my defense—but Flynn has gone to
procure a wagon and team. They were to deliver the powder
to Dublin today. I think—I think they intended to blow up
Dublin Castle, and then the wharves along the Liffey."

"I suppose that would make sense, from the
revolutionaries' perspective," Jamie said, nodding. "Move on
the castle, then take out the wharves and prevent any troops
from landing to put down the revolt."

"They won't do it with this powder, anyway," Pickett
observed breathlessly, glancing at all that remained of the
stockpile. "Still, I don't doubt Flynn will find himself a new
band of conspirators. Who knows? Someday they just might
succeed."

"You think Ireland will become a separate country
someday, like America?" asked Thomas, regarding his
employer curiously, as if wondering whether the stresses of
the previous days had been sufficient to disorder his senses.

"They keep—coming back," he pointed out, panting.
"No matter how many times they rebel—how harshly the

rebellion is put down—they keep coming back."

"What I'd like to know," Carson put in, returning to the subject at hand, "is why the devil didn't you shoot him, when you had the chance?"

Pickett looked at Julia, and although his face white and strained, his eyes were filled with love. "I didn't want to be like him."

"John!" she cried, her gratitude and relief quickly turning to dismay. "You're bleeding!"

"Yes—he got me—in the shoulder." Pickett observed with detached interest the blood that ran down his fingers and dripped onto the ground, collecting in a bright red pool at his feet. "It's all right—I'm perfectly fine—I'm—perfectly—"

Jamie caught him as he fell.

20

In Which John Pickett Must Make a Decision

W ell, I suppose this is it," Pickett said, turning away from the mirror with one last look at his reflection— or as much as he could see of it over Thomas, who hovered about giving one last-minute tweak to his cravat, brushing an imaginary speck of lint from the collar of his plum-colored coat, and, finally, straightening the folds of the cotton gauze looped about Pickett's neck, in which his left arm reposed. "The sling rather spoils the effect, doesn't it?"

"Not at all," protested Julia, to whom this query had been addressed. "You look quite heroic. And when one considers that you sustained the injury in uncovering a treasonous plot, well!—His Royal Highness can't help but be impressed. Am I not right, Thomas?"

"Aye, ma'am, that you are." There had been no further talk of putting his name forward at Bow Street, for since Pickett had been injured, Thomas had been in his element, having seized the rare opportunity to perform those tasks for his master that Pickett could not, at least for the nonce, perform for himself.

"Thank you, Thomas, that will be all," Pickett said in a voice that brooked no argument. Alone with Julia at last, he wrapped his good arm about her waist. "You're wrong on one point, you know. I sustained the injury in rescuing my wife," he said, punctuating this statement with a kiss.

"*You* know that, and *I* know that, but if the Prince of Wales chooses to believe otherwise, who are we to point out his error?" Her flirtatious smile faded, and she continued hesitantly, and in a more serious voice. "John, do you remember when we were in the Lake District, and you promised that whatever reward you received for the case would be mine to do with as I wished?"

"Yes, what of it?" She didn't answer at once, so he forced a smile and continued. "Although I'll admit that I was thinking of pounds sterling at the time. I never expected the reward to be anything like *this*."

"No." She blinked back the tears that never seemed to be far away these days, now that she was in the family way. "Nor did I."

"What's all this?" he asked in some alarm, releasing her in order to fumble in the breast pocket of his coat for a handkerchief. Finding what he sought, he shook it out and made an awkward, one-handed attempt at drying her tears.

"It's nothing." She took the handkerchief from him and finished the job properly. "I've become a veritable watering-pot lately! Please, pay me no heed. It's only that—John, darling, I'm so terribly proud of you. You know that, don't you?"

He knew, although he had no illusions as to his own worthiness to be held in such high regard. But because he loved her, he would do his best to try to deserve it, even if it meant giving up this place where they had been so happy. It was odd, in a way. Only a few months ago, he'd been intimidated by this tall, narrow house in Curzon Street, and wanted nothing more than to return to the shabby two-room flat in Drury Lane where they had spent the first week of their marriage. But at some point it had become home—*their* home, where they'd lived and loved and where, someday, their child would be born and would grow up.

Or so he'd imagined. Instead, they would have rooms in Carlton House, surrounded by the prince and his various sycophants, toadies, and hangers-on. He thought of the previous night, and the first opportunity he and Julia had had to mark their reunion. It had taken some imagination and not a little ingenuity, thanks to her increasing girth and his injured shoulder, and had been accompanied by a great deal of muffled laughter. There would be no such frolics at the royal residence, he was certain; no doubt the very walls of the royal residence would have ears, and however debauched the prince's own behavior, he would no doubt expect the comportment of those lesser mortals in his sphere to be above reproach. But it would be worth it, Pickett told himself firmly, to please this woman who had given up so much for his sake, and whom he had come so close to losing.

"Wish me luck," he said at last, drawing her back into the circle of his arm.

"You know I do," she said, and returned his kiss with feeling.

He had fully intended to walk to Pall Mall—after all, he walked much greater distances every day just going to Bow Street and back—but Julia, Rogers, and Thomas were all united against him: It would not do for him to appear at Carlton House with his cravat wilted and his face shiny with perspiration. And so Pickett, who knew a lost cause when he saw one, consented to being driven. Finding the carriage already at the door, he climbed inside and within minutes was set down in Pall Mall.

John Pickett was a tall young man, but as he passed between the Corinthian columns that fronted the portico, he felt distinctly small—a feeling that increased exponentially as he was admitted first to a foyer flanked by anterooms, then to an entrance hall with a skylight illuminating Ionic columns of yellow marble, and, finally, to an octagonal vestibule with doorways opening onto three of its eight sides, through one of which was visible a glimpse of a staircase. Here he was told he might wait while His Royal Highness was informed of Pickett's arrival.

As one minute stretched into two, and two into five, Pickett's curiosity overcame him. He crossed the room to the doorway on his right, any sound from his footsteps swallowed up by a carpet so thick that he would not have been surprised to look down and discover his feet sunk to the ankles. He peered through the doorway, and gazed upon the grandest staircase he had ever seen, a web of risers, treads, and gilded banisters that curved away out of sight in both directions.

"*Ahem!*" The rather pointed clearing of the footman's throat recalled Pickett to the purpose for which he had been summoned. "His Royal Highness will see you now. If you will follow me?"

He led Pickett through still more lavishly decorated rooms, glancing back from time to time as if to ensure that the visitor had not wandered off on an exploratory tour of the royal residence. At last they reached a room with crimson wall hangings and gilt-trimmed sofas and chairs. Reposing on one of the sofas was a stout man of middle age wearing a double-breasted blue tailcoat whose wide lapels bristled with medals. Pickett had never met the man, but he'd seen him once, through Julia's opera glasses, at Drury Lane Theatre, and so had no difficulty in recognizing George III's eldest son, the Prince of Wales. He took a deep breath and made what he hoped was a credible bow.

And in less than twenty minutes, the thing was done. As the front door closed behind him, Pickett stepped between the Corinthian columns out of the shadows of the portico and into the sunlight shining down on Pall Mall. Eschewing the carriage for the return trip, Pickett made the trek back to Curzon Street on foot, the better to ponder the conversation that had just taken place—and, perhaps, to delay the inevitable.

It was not Rogers who opened the door to him, but Julia, who had clearly been watching for his return.

"John!" she exclaimed, standing on tiptoe to kiss his cheek. "Back so soon? When are we to begin packing?"

"I—I turned it down," Pickett said dazedly, as if he could

not quite believe it himself.

She stared at him. "You—you—*what?*"

"I turned it down." He spoke more firmly this time, as if speaking the words aloud helped him to convince himself that they were true.

And then, to his abject horror, Julia buried her face in her hands and burst into tears—not the silent drops that sprang to her eyes so readily these days, but great wrenching sobs that shook her whole body.

"Julia—sweetheart—please—please don't cry," he begged, reaching for her with his good hand before thinking better of this gesture and letting it fall helplessly to his side. "I—I'm sorry—I hadn't meant to—I had every intention of— but when it came to the point, I just—I'm—I'm sorry."

Nothing he said had any effect except to make her cry still harder, so he tried a different tack. "I'll go back and tell him I changed my mind, shall I?" he offered in increasing desperation. Granted, he didn't hold out much hope for a second chance. By all accounts, Prinny was accustomed to getting his own way; certainly, he hadn't been at all pleased at having his generosity spurned, and certainly not by a creature of such humble origins as John Pickett, son of a convicted felon. "Maybe if I explain to him that I was overcome by the honor—I didn't know what I was saying—"

Julia's head shook vehemently from side to side. She swiped the tears from her face and looked up at him—and, incredibly, she was smiling. And not just any smile, but an expression of joy so radiant that it lit up her eyes and caused her wet cheeks to glow. "No—I'm sorry—it's just that—I'm just so glad!"

"*Glad?*" he echoed, stunned. "Do you mean—sweetheart, did you not *want* me to take it?"

"No—I should hate living at Carlton House! It is no place to raise a child, surrounded by the prince and his cronies—to say nothing of his mistresses! Then, too, the lack of—of privacy—" She colored slightly, giving Pickett to understand that she, too, had been thinking of the previous night's activities.

"But if you didn't want—Julia, why didn't you say so?" he asked, still struggling to take it in. "I told you any reward I received from the business in the Lake District was yours to do with as you pleased; did you not believe me?"

"Yes, but how could I ask you to refuse such an honor? You may say you don't deserve it, but I know better!" She added, more hesitantly, "I know, too, how much you hate being my—my pensioner."

"It bothers me, if I allow myself to dwell on it," Pickett admitted, "but if you want to know the truth, I haven't thought of it in a very long time."

Julia cocked one eyebrow skeptically. "Not even when you were offered five hundred per annum?"

"No. Well, perhaps a little," he confessed. "But it had nothing to do with my no longer being dependent on your jointure from your first husband. It was more about the baby, and the fact that if we were able to live on my salary, then we could save your money for the baby's schooling if it's a boy, or dowry if it's a girl."

"Then—you never really *wanted* to accept the prince's

offer?"

"No! Oh, I was flattered, I'll not deny that, but my only reason for even considering it was the prospect of giving you back some measure of the position in society that you lost when you married me."

She thought of the disastrous tea party, and the guests who had snubbed her, and how unimportant it all seemed, in the light of everything that had happened since then. "Emily Dunnington once told me that the ladies of the *ton* don't snub me because I married you; they snub me because I'm happy with you, that I remind them of the fact that they made compromises by marrying for the sake of a title, or a fortune, or an exalted connection, and now have to live with the consequences. I don't know if she's right or not, but I know that as long as I have you, I don't care about anyone else—certainly not the sort of people who would be impressed by my close proximity to the prince's Carlton House set!" For a moment she feared that she had said too much, that he would remember he'd left her on the brink of hosting a tea party, and would ask about it.

But she need not have worried, for he was lost in thoughts of his own. He wrapped his good arm about her waist and drew her close, bending his head to rest his cheek against her golden curls. He had declined the position offered by the Prince of Wales, but he would have to leave Bow Street all the same. His duties there as a principal officer made it almost inevitable that there would be angry, resentful men looking for retribution against the one responsible for their own incarceration, or the transportation or even the execution of their friends or family members. What better revenge against him than to harm or even kill those he loved? He had managed to save her this time, but what about the next time? Or the next?

No, he would not put Julia in danger again. And so, as soon as his shoulder was healed and his arm was free of its confounded sling, he would find a new situation, something reasonably respectable—a bank clerk, perhaps, or under-secretary for an insurance firm. Deadly dull, perhaps, but undeniably safe.

And, after obtaining such a post, he would resign his position at Bow Street.

About the Author

At the age of sixteen, Sheri Cobb South discovered Georgette Heyer, and came to the startling realization that she had been born into the wrong century. Although she probably would have been a chambermaid had she actually lived in Regency England, that didn't stop her from fantasizing about waltzing the night away in the arms of a handsome, wealthy, and titled gentleman.

Since Georgette Heyer died in 1974 and could not write any more Regencies, Ms. South came to the conclusion she would have to do it herself. In addition to the bestselling John Pickett mystery series (now an award-winning audiobook series!), she has also written several Regency romances, including the critically acclaimed *The Weaver Takes a Wife*.

A native and long-time resident of Alabama, Ms. South now lives in Loveland, Colorado.

She loves to hear from readers, and invites them to visit her website at www.shericobbsouth.com; follow her on social media through Facebook, Goodreads, Pinterest, Instagram, or Twitter; or email her at Cobbsouth@aol.com.

Made in the USA
Monee, IL
08 December 2019